Speaking of Snapdragons

SPEAKING OF SNAP- DRAGONS

SHEILA HAYES

LODESTAR BOOKS

E. P. Dutton • New York

LIBRARY OF CONGRESS CATALOGING IN PUBLICATION DATA
Hayes, Sheila.
Speaking of snapdragons.

Summary: During the summer while she is on her own,
eleven-year-old Heather forms a friendship with an old,
reclusive man who spends his days tending his garden.
[1. Friendship—Fiction.   2. Old age—Fiction.
3. Single-parent family—Fiction.   4. Gardening—
Fiction]   I. Title.
PZ7.H314874Sp 1982   [Fic]   82-9901
ISBN 0-525-66785-7   AACR2

Published in the United States by E. P. Dutton, Inc.,
2 Park Avenue, New York, N.Y. 10016
Published simultaneously in Canada by Clarke,
Irwin & Company Limited, Toronto and Vancouver
Editor: Virginia Buckley   Designer: Trish Parcell
Printed in the U.S.A.   First Edition
10   9   8   7   6   5   4   3   2   1

To my mother
and the memory of my father

Contents

Speaking of Snapdragons

1

So Long, Marshall

I certainly don't envy Marshall getting Herb Teitelbaum for a father. Not that he's *grotesque* or anything like that. In fact, if he had always been around, if he had taken Marshall home from the hospital and been his father right from the very beginning, he would probably have seemed terrific. But if you're a kid like Marshall and me, *fatherless* as they say in those magazine articles, and you were suddenly going to get a father, I think you could do a lot better than Herb Teitelbaum.

I didn't say that to Marshall, of course. When he finally told us about his mother getting married again, it was the Friday before the wedding and I was standing in line at the milk counter with all the other kids. I think I said something like "That's nice" or "Gee, that's great, Marshall," and I never let on that I wasn't a bit surprised.

I had known about Marshall's mother getting married weeks ago. My mom is a good friend of his mom, so she had heard about it and she tells me everything. I was really hurt

3

that Marshall didn't mention it to me ahead of time. We've been best friends since nursery school, and even if nobody in sixth grade realizes that we're still best friends, even if everybody thinks his best friend is Ricky Schneider and my best friend is Lisa Pringle, *he* knows different and he should have told me.

After the big announcement, when Lisa and I had settled at our lunch table, I said, "I certainly wouldn't want Mr. Teitelbaum for a father."

She took a bite out of her tuna fish sandwich and then waited until she had chewed and swallowed every bit of it before she answered me. Sometimes I think she does that just to aggravate me.

"Why not?" she asked.

"Well, for one thing, he's almost bald."

"So what?"

I stared at her. "That's easy for you to say. Your father has all that curly hair."

Lisa made a face. "Sometimes, Heather, you are so *strange*. It doesn't make any difference how much hair he has. I think it's wonderful that Marshall's going to have a real father."

She stopped then, and I watched her as she picked up crumbs with her fingertip. She was feeling sorry for me again, I could tell. I can't stand it when people feel sorry for me.

When Lisa Pringle first decided that we should be best friends, I was thrilled. Lisa doesn't live in the condominiums with Marshall and me. She lives in a big white colonial about five blocks away. There are four kids in the Pringle family

4

(two boys and two girls), they have three cars, and her father's a doctor and also President of the Oakfield Board of Education. As if that isn't enough, Lisa's very pretty, with long blonde hair that she wears in lots of different styles. She also has more clothes than any other girl in the class. So you can see how I felt: If I *had* to have a girl for a best friend, I was lucky to have someone like Lisa.

I rolled up my lunch bag and stood up. "Well, all I know is, I'd hate to have a bald, middle-aged man hanging around all the time. It'd drive me crazy! See you outside," I said.

I ran over to the jungle gym and climbed to the top so fast I was almost out of breath. The air was thick with spring as I straddled the top bar and looked down, watching the kids as they came out of the lunchroom. I loved sitting up high like that. It made me feel so free.

Marshall and Ricky came running out. Marsh was always easy to spot, with his thatch of strawlike hair and his glasses sliding down his nose. I remember when he first got his glasses. We were in kindergarten, and one of the boys said he looked like an owl and made him cry. He *did* look like an owl, exactly like the Wise potato chip owl, but I punched the kid anyway.

Ever since my mom told me she thought Mrs. Benedict was going to "remarry" as she put it, I've had this queer feeling in the pit of my stomach. I keep remembering things. Not just about the glasses, but how I didn't feel so bad not having a father for Brownie father/daughter night, because Marshall didn't have one for Cub Scout father/son night. Now anytime he needed a father for something, he'd have one. I wonder if Mr. Teitelbaum will adopt Marshall, and he'll be Marshall Teitelbaum instead of Marshall Benedict. All my life he's been Marshall Benedict, right next door with his mom. Just the two of them and the two of us . . .

Lisa was standing at the foot of the jungle gym looking up at me.

"We're going to play baseball with some of the guys. You wanna come over?"

I hesitated a moment. I felt so sad suddenly that I thought I'd burst. Then I took a deep breath—that helps sometimes.

"Sure," I said, and scrambled back down to the ground.

The game was fun. I don't think Marsh had to laugh quite so loud when Petey hit me in the ribs as I slid into third, but that's the way it is when the other kids are around. I don't call him Four-eyes the way Brucie does, but I call him Marshmallow and dummy and regular things like that.

By the time we went in to social studies, I felt fine again.

When I got home from school, there were some neat things in the mail. There were two catalogs from garden centers and one from a gift shop in Minnesota. I don't know how these places get our name, but I'm glad they do. It makes the mail more interesting. There were a couple of bills, too, and I *know* how those people got our name. We owe Burden's Department Store a lot of money because we just got new slipcovers. And the insurance on the car is due, too. But I decided not to think about that now.

Tiger followed me into the kitchen. His small, furry body was trembling, and he was whimpering the way he does every afternoon when I get home from school. I guess he gets lonesome being stuck in the house by himself all day. I took a cupcake for myself and a dog biscuit for Tiger, and then the two of us lay on the living-room rug while I looked at one of the garden catalogs.

One of the ads said:

> Be the envy of all your friends with this four foot tall banana tree *growing right in your own living room!* Just think how they'll stare, *wonder* in their eyes, as you casually stroll over to your very own banana tree and pick a nice, ripe banana. How *grateful* they'll be if you offer them one! How *eager* they'll be to learn the secret of your botanical magic! How . . .

I turned the page. How stupid did they think I was? What kind of weirdo would have a banana tree growing in the middle of their living room? Tarzan, maybe. I looked at the cover of the catalog. It was a company I'd never heard of, so I tossed it down and picked up the next one. This was more like it. I looked at the pictures of zinnias and delphiniums, asters and marigolds. . . . I love even the *names* of flowers.

I would love to have a garden. Lisa's folks have lots of property, and they have flowers all over their backyard. They even grow their own vegetables. I'd be happy if just one thing I planted bloomed. If there's really something called a green thumb, I think I must have a purple one. And Mom says *she* doesn't have the time, and besides, we don't have the space. The condominiums are attached to each other, and each one has a patio and a little patch of green in the back. But how much space would a few flowers need? I've seen photos of this place when my folks first bought it,

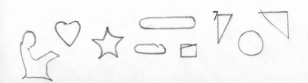

and there were flowers in the back. Of course, that was when I was a baby. My dad died when I was three, and the backyard's been pretty bleak ever since.

I wondered suddenly if Mr. Teitelbaum was a gardener. Or if Marshall's mom wouldn't go to work anymore and would stay home all day growing flowers like Mrs. Pringle. It was going to happen so soon. Sunday—bingo!—Marshall would have a father.

I jumped up and went into the kitchen. Mom had left some hamburger thawing on the counter. What could I do with it that would be creative? Meat loaf. I'd make a meat loaf. I am undoubtedly one of the best eleven-year-old cooks you'll ever meet. That's why Mom and I don't need anyone else around. I can do everything she can do. Except, maybe, run a gift shop like The Treasure Chest.

I heard the key in the lock at 5:45 exactly.

"Hi, Mom. How was your day?"

"Fine, honey," she said, kicking off her shoes and flipping through the mail.

"The car insurance came in. Don't forget to pay it. We don't want to have to pay a late penalty again."

"Yes, ma'am! What smells so good?"

"Meat loaf. Meat loaf and scalloped potatoes."

"Terrific. I'm starved."

"Well, then, wash up. It's almost ready."

I had put too much salt in the potatoes, but otherwise everything was pretty good. Mom says it's progress when you know when you've messed up something. Some nights I make better progress than others.

"Mom, did you see the catalogs that came in the mail?"

"Hmm . . ." she said, not lifting her eyes from the editorial page of the *Oakfield Tribune.*

"I think I'm going to try a garden again."

She lowered the paper and stared at me. "I'll give you credit for one thing. You're persistent."

"Well, I'm learning. Wouldn't you *like* to have flowers out there?"

"I would love to. But I can't grow a thing, and neither can you."

"That's not fair. Daddy was a gardener. Maybe I take after him."

Mom lowered the newspaper again. "Your red hair you got from your father, but that's all."

"Well, I can try, can't I?"

"Sure. Just don't get anything that costs too much. And remember, we have a very small backyard."

Mom cleared and did the dishes. That's our agreement. One of us cooks; the other clears. I heard a lady tell Mom once that we were more like roommates than mother and daughter, and I think that's true.

Since it was Friday, there was no big hurry to do my homework, so I decided to call Lisa and see if she'd go to Brockmeyer's with me tomorrow.

The Pringle house is so *noisy*, but I guess that's what it's like when you have four kids in a family. I had to shout to be heard over the din in the background when Lisa's brother finally got her to the phone.

"Guess what?" I said.

"Barry Sawyer asked you to marry him!"

"Shut up!" I yelled. "How gross. I'd die before I'd marry him."

"Sure you would. Of happiness . . ." she said in a singsong voice.

"Li-sa! I'm never going to tell you anything ever again. Besides, I don't even like him anymore."

"Okay, okay. So what's up?"

"I'm going to have a garden!"

"Again?"

"You don't have to put it that way. This is the time of year lots of people start gardens."

"Yeah, but not *you*, Heather. You know you can't grow a thing. Why don't you just let me give you some flowers from our garden, like I did last year?"

"That's not the same, Lisa. I want to grow my own. I like to make things."

I could hear this real patient sigh on the other end of the phone.

"Okay, if you want to waste your time."

"Gee, thanks a lot. I can always depend on you to make me feel really great. You don't have to go with me then, okay?"

"Go with you where?"

"To Brockmeyer's to get some little plants and things."

"Oh . . . when did you want to go?"

"Tomorrow."

"Do you want my mom to drive us?"

"No, let's just walk, okay? It's not that far."

"I dunno. I'll have to ask. Wait a minute," and I heard the

phone drop with a thud as she ran off screaming "Moth-er!" at the top of her lungs.

Lisa's mother drives her everywhere. I think if she's in the kitchen and she has to go to the john, her mother drives her.

Finally she got back on the phone. "I can go, but my mother's not too thrilled about it."

"Lisa, it's not that far."

"Yeah, but there's Russell Square to cross."

"You can hold my hand, okay?"

"Very funny. You'll pick me up?"

"Yeah. How about ten o'clock?"

"Okay. See ya."

"Bye."

I was sitting there trying to remember what was on television, and being too lazy to go find the TV listing, when the phone rang.

"Hello."

"Hi."

"Hi, Marsh. How ya doing?"

"Okay. Know what's on Channel 7 tonight? *Godzilla!*"

"You're kidding!" Marshall and I watched *Godzilla* one night when we were little and he was sleeping over (our mothers used to do that a lot so they didn't have to get a baby-sitter). Anyway, it was so scary that we woke up my mom and got into trouble because we were supposed to be asleep already. She yelled at us a lot, and then she let us get into bed with her.

"You going to watch it?" I asked.

"Sure, I'm not chicken. Listen, Heather, I got a favor to ask."

"What is it?"

"You know how I'm staying at Ricky's while my mom goes away . . . you know, after she gets married?"

"Yeah, I know." I noticed Marshall didn't say *honeymoon* and I was glad he didn't. It's such an icky word.

"Well, Mrs. Schneider won't let me bring Peanut Butter and Jelly with me. She's afraid their cat will get at them. Will you keep them for me?"

"Sure I will. I'd love it!" Peanut Butter and Jelly are Marshall's gerbils. We named them that because Peanut Butter and Jelly are the two things Marshall loves most in the whole world. I didn't know how keen my mother would be about it, but I knew she'd want to help Mrs. Benedict.

"I'll bring them over tomorrow afternoon, okay?"

"Okay." I was going to tell Marshall about starting a garden again, but I decided not to. Let him be surprised when my backyard was the riot of color those catalogs were always promising. Anyway, I decided I'd better say something about his mother marrying Mr. Teitelbaum. "I guess you're excited about the wedding," I said.

"Yep. You should see the cake they ordered. Did I tell you Herb's got a camper, and we're going camping as soon as school is out?"

"No, you didn't." The truth is, I had sort of avoided the subject of Mr. Teitelbaum whenever we were together. And Marshall's not telling anyone about the wedding until today made me wonder just how thrilled he was with the whole idea. Suddenly I realized how strange it must be for Marsh, and I wanted to say something to make him feel good.

"I think you're very lucky to be getting such a nice . . . uh . . . stepfather," I said stiffly.

But all he said was, "I sure am. Remember, *Godzilla*, nine o'clock, Channel 7. So long."

"So long, Marshall," I said.

I tried watching *Godzilla*, but it wasn't scary anymore. I couldn't concentrate anyway. Somehow I couldn't shake the dumb feeling that it really was "So long, Marshall."

2
The Old Man

I love the way Brockmeyer's smells. It's a big garden center on the outskirts of town, and when we were little, Mom and Mrs. Benedict used to take Marshall and me to see Santa Claus at Brockmeyer's every Christmas, when they convert one of the sheds into Santa's workshop. I never really believed in Santa Claus, of course, because my mother doesn't go for that sort of thing, but it was fun just to see somebody dressed up in a Santa costume. When I sat on his lap, I used to try and figure out how he kept his false beard on. Marshall always asked for every single toy he saw advertised on television. I only asked for the ones I knew Mom could buy me. That way I was never disappointed.

Anyway, I still remember the smell of the animals and the pine needles. Now it was May and the scent of lilacs filled the air.

"Look at these," Lisa said, pointing to some absolutely gorgeous pink flowers tumbling out of wooden tubs at the entrance.

I stopped to read the tag. *Tuberose Begonias*, it said. I let myself imagine for a moment how great they would look by our back door. But with the tub, they were much too expensive.

"Too *showy*," I said to Lisa, brushing past them and going inside.

"Then how about some of the grape hyacinths?" she asked, making her way past pots of tulips and daffodils to where the tiny purple flowers were clustered at the farthest corner of the spring planting section.

"But they're so little," I said.

"Well . . ." but then Lisa just shrugged her shoulders as if she had decided not to say what she was thinking.

"My backyard is not *that* small," I snapped. I turned to go down a path lined with bright pink azalea bushes, when Lisa pulled me back.

"Watch it," she hissed.

"What's the matter?"

"Look who's over there."

I looked to where she nodded and saw a stooped figure in a battered hat and a cardigan sweater that was about two sizes too big for him.

"It's the old man," I said.

"I thought he was *dead* by now," she said.

"No, I see him once in a while."

"You do? Oh sure, you live near him. I'm sure glad I don't. He gives me the creeps."

"Oh, *Lisa*," I heard myself sigh, as I stopped and watched him for a moment. He was shuffling along slowly, bending over from time to time to sniff a flower or touch a leaf. He actually seemed to be having a *conversation* with some of the plants. I tugged at Lisa's sleeve, and we started down the next aisle.

The old man, as the kids call him, lives in a big white farmhouse that sits on a hill at one end of Cardigan Corners, where Marshall and I live. The farmhouse used to belong to the people who owned the land where our condominiums are now. I've heard that when the old man bought the house, some kids went trick-or-treating there one Halloween, and he scared the daylights out of them. Kids say there were bats flying around the place, just like a horror movie. I don't know what happened. I was only a baby then. But ever since, people stay away from the house. And ever since, Thomas Worthington Duffy doesn't go near anybody.

I was the one who discovered his real name. We got some of his mail by mistake, and that was the name on the envelope. My mother said he was quite a successful man at one time, but now he's what they call a *recluse*. I think that's something like a hermit without a beard.

"Come on," I said to Lisa, who kept turning to stare at him. "I still have to get my flowers." But the more I looked at the prices, the more discouraged I was getting. But to Lisa all I said was, "I can't make up my mind."

"Listen, I have to pick up a pair of garden gloves for my mother, and I have to get back to go to the dentist, so why don't I meet you at the cashier?"

"Okay," I said, waving her away and watching her go inside the red barn where they sold tools and equipment. I stood trying to decide between five daffodils or four tulips. Either way, I wasn't going to get much for my money.

"What I need is a *lot* of something for a *little* money. And it has to grow right away," I said out loud, to nobody in particular.

But somebody in particular answered me.

"Impatient," I heard somebody mumble behind me. I turned and almost jumped out of my skin.

He was standing about two inches away from me, wearing a pair of worn-looking trousers and a faded blue work shirt, which, like the cardigan sweater, looked much too big for him. His battered hat was pulled down over a face as pink and wrinkled as a newborn baby's, but he peered out at me with eyes that were amazingly clear and blue. I was face to face with the old man.

"Ex—excuse me," I said. "I guess I am sort of impatient."

He shook his head from side to side, and he was so frail that for a moment I was worried it was going to roll off his shoulders.

"Not impatient, *impatiens*," he said, looking annoyed. I caught a fresh smell of soap as he brushed past me and pointed over to the left of where we were standing. "Busy Lizzies is their nickname."

Turning, I saw rows and rows of lovely little flowers in every shade of pink from pale to rose to red. I went over to look at the price tag. They were the cheapest plants I had seen.

"They are lovely," I said.

"Of course they are. Why would you want daffodils and tulips? They'll be gone in no time. Separate these and you'll get six good plants out of a box. And they'll spread and grow like a brush fire." His bright blue eyes fixed on me intently, and I knew he was waiting for my decision. What would happen, I wondered nervously, if I ignored his advice?

I looked back at the impatiens. "They *are* beautiful. . . . And I could take two boxes of them. Six plants in each . . . that means I could plant twelve of them."

Out of the corner of my eye I could see Lisa looking for me. What would she think when she saw me talking to the old man? I waved to her and then scooped up a box of the pale pink and a box of the deep pink. "Thank you," I said and hurried over to where Lisa was standing with her mouth hanging open.

"My gosh, you talked to him. . . ."

"Come on, let's get out to the cashier."

"But you talked to the old man! Was he as weird as they say? Were you scared?"

"Well, I was a little," I began. Lisa's reaction pleased me. It wasn't often I did something that impressed her.

"What did he *say* to you?"

"Uh, well, he just mumbled something at first. I wasn't sure what it was. . . ."

"Then what happened?"

I looked down at the lovely pink flowers I was holding, and my conscience bothered me.

"He told me I should buy these flowers," I said.

"Did he force you? Did he threaten you?" Lisa's eyes bulged.

"No, Lisa, not really. Oh gosh, Lisa," I said, mumbling myself at this point, "he's just an old man."

"Just an old man! Not on Halloween, he isn't. You were lucky to get away in one piece, Heather. Boy, if I tell my mother about this, she'll never let me come here again. This must be where he hangs out."

"Lisa," I said, "just be quiet a minute, okay?" I was up to the cashier by now, and I was trying to count my money. "Here," I said, handing her one of the boxes, "can you carry one of these?"

"But I have these to carry," she said, waving a minuscule paper bag in one hand.

"What are those, the gloves?"

"Yep."

"They must weigh a ton."

She looked at me and made a face. "All right," she said, "gimme," and she took one of the boxes as we started home.

The impatiens weren't heavy, but I wanted to be careful carrying them. I didn't want to damage a single leaf.

"I think we have some of these," Lisa said, looking down and sniffing the plants.

"Is there any flower in the whole world that you don't have?" I asked, trying not to be annoyed.

"Oh come on," she said, with exaggerated modesty, "our garden's *nothing* compared to my grandmother's. She's the one who was written up in the paper last year. Did I tell you about her roses?"

"Yeah, you did," I said.

"Does your grandmother have a garden?" she asked.

I looked over at her. "Lisa, my grandmother lives on the twelfth floor of an apartment building in Chicago. You know that! How could she have a garden? She might have some houseplants, though. . . . I'll have to ask her the next time she calls."

"Don't you miss having her around?"

"Yeah, I do. But she has a good job in Chicago, and she's happy there. And we're happy here. She stayed with us for a while, you know, when I was little, after my dad died. But she has a different kind of life than we do, and Mom says it's better if people are independent and live their own lives." We walked along in silence for a moment, and then a happy thought crossed my mind. "Did I tell you she may come for a visit?"

"No, you didn't! When?"

"I'm not sure. I *hope* this summer. She's very busy, so she kind of squeezes us in."

"I'm going to my grandparents' for the whole month of July this year."

I looked over at her, stricken. "You never go for that long! How come you're going for a whole month?"

"I think my mom wants to get rid of me," she giggled. "The boys are getting so rough, and we fight a lot. Besides, my cousin Barbara's going to be there the same time. It's going to be neat. It's such a big place, and there's always something going on. What are you going to do when school gets out?"

I felt a little quiver of fear when she asked the question. It was something I was trying not to think about. Summers had always been a lazy time, and even if Lisa was away and Ricky and all the other kids, I had Marshall to do things with. Now he'd be away camping with old Herb.

"I may go to day camp, I'm not sure. Or take a course at the summer workshop. There's some neat things this year.

And there'll be lots of girls around." I hoped I sounded more enthusiastic than I felt.

"You'll probably get an invitation to Emily Leonard's birthday party. I told her I couldn't go because I was going to be away, so I think she'll invite you instead."

I glanced sideways at Lisa, but she was just loping along, humming under her breath. I know she doesn't mean to hurt my feelings the way she does. I try to remember that. And most of the time she's fun. It's only sometimes, like now, that she gets on my nerves.

A cat ran across the street in front of us, and for some reason that made me think of Marshall's gerbils. I still hadn't told my mother they were coming.

"Guess what?" I said, "I'm taking care of Marshall's gerbils while he stays at Ricky's house."

"Oh, luck-y! I'd love to have gerbils. But where are you going to keep them so Tiger doesn't get at them?"

"Lisa, Tiger's a dog. He can't get at them the way a cat can."

"Remember last year when Jamie took care of the class gerbils, and his dog ate one of them?"

"Ugh. Don't remind me. But that was a German shepherd. Tiger's such a little thing. He can't get up very high. I'll just keep them up on a shelf."

When we got to Hobson Street, Lisa handed me my plants, said "Call me," and ran across a wide sweep of lawn littered with tricycles and pull toys. I continued down the road until I came to Lehigh Street, and the fourth condominium on the left. But I didn't go up our driveway right away. I stood for a moment looking down the street toward the dead end, where the Duffy house perched on a hill. You couldn't see the house until you were practically *in* the house, because of all the trees around it. But suddenly I was aware of it, and of the person who lived there.

It took me all afternoon to get my twelve impatiens plants into the ground, but I enjoyed doing it. This was one of the Saturdays Mom had to work, so I was glad for something to do besides the laundry.

I placed rocks here and there between the plants to make it look like a rock garden. When I was finished I stepped back and admired what I had done. Then I went in and made myself a peanut butter and jelly sandwich. That's when I remembered the gerbils again. Where was I going to put them?

I looked around the living room. The gerbil cage was large, not the kind of thing you could stick in an out-of-the-way place and ignore. I thought of my room. But the idea of the two little things scratching around in the middle of the night made me kind of itchy. The bathroom was too small. . . .

It was almost five o'clock when Marshall came to the back door with the large gerbil cage in his arms. Luckily, Mom wasn't home yet. I helped Marsh set it down in the place I had chosen.

"Here's the food, Heather. Feed them every morning, don't forget. And keep the tube filled with water." Then, to the two tiny animals he said, "So long, you guys."

"You can come over after school to visit them if you want."

"Naw, I don't think Ricky would want to. You know . . ."

"Yeah, I know. He thinks his ears'll fall off if he comes in a girl's house."

"I gotta go. See ya."

"So long. Oh, and Marshall . . . uh . . . have a nice time at the wedding tomorrow."

"Yeah . . . thanks."

I closed the back door and was just starting a conversation with Peanut Butter and Jelly when I heard my mother come in the front.

"Hi!" I said brightly. "How was work?"

"Same as always," she said.

She was obviously not in the best possible mood to learn that we had two uninvited houseguests, so I waited, hoping for just the right moment to break the news. But I waited a moment too long. She was on her way through to the kitchen, when I heard a bloodcurdling scream.

"Heath-er! There are *rats* in the middle of the dinette table!"

For some reason, whenever I'm in trouble, I talk fast.

"Mom, I read this article in *Better Homes & Gardens*— or was it *House & Garden*?—anyway, it said you should be creative when it comes to a centerpiece for your dinner table. *Anybody* can just stick a bowl of fruit or some flowers down in the middle of things and call that a center-piece, but the truly creative person tries to make a state-ment."

"Heather!"

"They're just gerbils, Mom. Marshall's gerbils. I didn't think you'd mind."

"But the dinette table—that's disgusting!"

"I thought it made a statement about loving animals."

"They make me itch just looking at them."

"You *do* love animals, don't you?"

"They make me feel dirty."

"You always said you loved animals."

"You'll just have to put them somewhere else," my mother said firmly, scratching herself as she hurried away.

"Some animal lover you turned out to be!" I yelled after her. But by this time she was in the shower, and I don't think she heard me.

3

Opposite Sides

According to my mother, the wedding was lovely. I wouldn't know, of course, since I wasn't invited. Mom said it was just family and close friends and Marshall, who seemed a little uncomfortable about being the only child there. Mom also said that old Herb looked very nice in a blue suit with a blue polka-dot tie. I'm sure he would have looked even nicer in a toupee.

For the next couple of weeks, I found myself staring at Marshall from time to time, trying to see if he was any different. Which I *knew* was ridiculous. After all, how could he be any different? He didn't get Superman for a father.

Unfortunately, no one had told Marshall that he hadn't gotten Superman for a father. Our conversations went something like this:

"Did I tell you about the neat camper Herb's got? We're going camping as soon as school is out."

"Yes, Marsh, you told me."

"Did I tell you Herb's gonna coach a soccer team in the fall?"

"Yes, Marsh, you told me."

"Did I tell you Herb used to be a lifeguard? He's gonna teach me how to dive."

"Yes, Marsh, you told me."

Did I tell you he can leap tall buildings in a single bound? Yes, Marsh, you told me. . . .

Field Day is always a big event on the last Wednesday of the school year. We have races and games, and afterward, hot dogs and soda. Parents are invited, and some of them come (the ones who have nothing else to do all day, like Lisa's mother). But Marshall's mom could never come, nor could mine, and we didn't care. We competed for *ourselves*, and when it was over, any ribbons that we'd won could be brought home and shown off at the dinner table.

The morning of Field Day was cloudy and cool, but by ten o'clock, when the games started, the sun began to peek through and we knew we'd have a great day for the games.

Our grade was divided, as always, between the Blues and the Yellows. Marshall and Lisa were both on the Blue team while I was on the Yellow with Ricky and Deirdre, two of the best athletes in sixth grade. Marshall and I usually try to manage it so that at some point we're opposite each other in a race. I'm taller than he is, but skinnier, so I think it works out even.

This year we weren't up against each other until the potato race, and by that time the score was tied, 12–12. We were both the last in our line, and Deirdre handed me the spoon a split second before Billy gave Marshall his. I started out as fast as I could, and I was almost at the end, with Marshall just two or three steps behind me, when I heard this voice loud and clear from the parents' section.

"Come on, Marshall, you can catch her!"

I looked up to see who it was, and in that instant, as I caught sight of Herb Teitelbaum's bald head, Marshall lunged past me to the finish line.

"Why did you stop?" Penny said to me, obviously annoyed. "Now the Blues are ahead 14–12!"

I glared at Marshall. "I don't think it's fair to have people call out and try to distract you. That's the same as cheating."

"Are you saying I cheat?" Marshall yelled back.

"I'm not saying anything. Except everybody here knows who should have won that race."

"Sore loser, sore loser!" It was Lisa. I wanted to kill her.

"Parents are allowed to cheer their kids on, Heather. Or don't you know that?" Marshall said venomously.

"Most fathers," I said, "are at work during the day." My throat was beginning to feel hot and dry. I was sorry I had started this whole conversation.

"Herb has his own business so he can do anything he wants, stupid," he said, and then he turned and stomped over to where the Blues were lining up for the three-legged race.

I don't think I'd ever been so mad at Marshall. To think that I had let his gerbils keep me awake every night for a week! We had been on opposite sides lots of times, and we had never had any trouble. But now we were on opposite sides in a different way.

I was Ricky's partner in the three-legged race. Once again I was against Marshall, who had Lisa as his partner.

"Come on," I said to Ricky, as we tied the piece of cloth around our ankles. "We've got to beat them."

Billy and Deirdre were faster than Tom and Molly, so we started off several steps ahead.

"Come *on!*" I kept saying to Ricky, as if I could somehow propel both of us through the air to the finish line. But I was so busy urging Ricky to "come on" that I didn't see the rut in the dirt. My ankle turned and I went down, bringing Ricky down on top of me. As I sat there, hurting and catching my breath, I could hear a voice yelling, "Nice going, Marshall. Keep it up!"

We were behind by four points now, and unless Marshall broke his leg, I knew we weren't going to beat them. I was right. The Blues beat us in the sack race, and even though we won the relay, they came out ahead. Maybe they would have beaten us anyway, but Herb Teitelbaum cheering them on didn't seem quite fair.

When we had our hot dogs and Cokes, I avoided Lisa and Marshall and sat with Deirdre and Molly.

"Don't be a sore loser. Come on, cheer up!" Lisa said, coming over and plopping herself down where she wasn't welcome.

"I am *not* a sore loser," I said between clenched teeth. "Stop saying that!"

"Well then, what's wrong with you? Nobody tripped you, you know. You'd think it was my fault the Blues beat the Yellows!" And she jumped up and went back to the other side of the field.

"Nobody thinks it's your fault," Deirdre said quietly. She was trying to be nice, I knew that. But I didn't want anybody to be nice to me. I just glared at her, and when they were finished eating, she and Molly got up and left.

I sat by myself feeling miserable until the whistle blew. This whole messy day was proof that things had changed forever between Marshall and me.

I was still in a rotten mood when I got home from school. Here it was, practically summer vacation, and for the first time in my life I wasn't even looking forward to it. What was there to look forward to? Lisa was going away for a month to her grandparents' (where there was a lake the size of the Atlantic Ocean), and I was never going to speak to Marshall again, *ever*. Which would put a dent in our friendship even if he wasn't going to spend the whole summer flying around with Superdad.

There was an invitation to Emily Leonard's birthday party in the mail, but since I knew why I had been invited, it didn't do much toward cheering me up.

I was sitting in the kitchen, digging a huge hole to crawl into, when I saw it. I must have carried it in with the rest of the mail, but in my black mood I hadn't even noticed. It was a medium-sized manila envelope, kind of puffy, as if it was stuffed with something. It was addressed in big bold letters:

MISS HEATHER MALLORY
16 LEHIGH STREET
OAKFIELD, OHIO

I picked it up and read the return address:

MILLICENT HAMILTON
2331 LAKE SHORE DRIVE
CHICAGO, ILLINOIS

It was from my grandmother! But what would she be sending me? And why? It wasn't even my birthday.

I ripped open the envelope and pulled out something blue wrapped in tissue paper. It was a T-shirt, and on the front it had a big yellow daisy with the words *Flower Power*. Quickly I pulled off my blouse and tried it on. A perfect fit. A note fell to the ground, and I picked it up. FROM THE DESK OF . . . MILLIE HAMILTON it said on top. I read,

> *Dear Heather,*
>
> *Your mother tells me you've become a gardener, so when I saw this T-shirt, I immediately thought of you. I'm so sorry I won't see you in it this summer but things are madness here! Maybe in the fall?*
>
> *Love and kisses,*
Grandma

When I finished reading the note, I felt as if I had a big rock inside my chest. But I wasn't really surprised. Mom's taught me never, ever to count on something, or take it for granted that something good is going to happen. That way you're never disappointed. But it seems to me that counting on something, looking forward to something, is half the fun. How come Marshall can count on things? And Lisa? She counts on things more than anybody I know!

I went over and looked at myself in the mirror. Not bad. When I got a tan this summer, and all the freckles blended together, the T-shirt would look great.

I filled the watering can and went outside to water my flowers.

"See my new T-shirt?" I said. "My grandmother sent it to me from Chicago." I had read somewhere that you should talk to plants to make them grow. The article meant houseplants, but I figure a plant is a plant. I suddenly realized that if anybody was watching me, I must look as loony as the old man did in Brockmeyer's.

I knelt down to take a close look at my impatiens. Three had toppled over dead, as if they had been shot, as soon as they were planted. Two were sprouting new buds, but the others seemed to have gone into a coma. They weren't wilting, but they weren't thriving either. It was as if they were waiting for their orders: Should they live or die? *"Live! Live!"* I yelled at them. Tiger had followed me out, and he stood, his head cocked to one side listening. Obviously he thought I was talking to him. Who else was around?

"This is going to be my gardening T-shirt," I said. "When they come to photograph me for the gardening section of the Sunday paper, I will wear this T-shirt and look terrific. Everyone will say, 'What a magnificent garden! And what a magnificent tan! She must get that magnificent tan working all day in that magnificent garden!'"

I kept on this way for a while, and pretty soon I was feeling fine again. So what if my grandmother wasn't coming? So what if Marsh was gone forever? So what if Lisa went away for a month? There were lots of other kids around.

When I went to Emily Leonard's party, there'd be lots of *super* kids there, and we'd make *super* plans to do lots of *super* things this summer!

When Mom came home, I showed her the Flower Power T-shirt.

"That was nice of her," she said, reading the note and letting it fall to the table. "And *you* seem to be in a good mood!"

"I am," I said, setting the table.

"Then I take it for granted you won today," she said, going in to change her clothes.

I dropped the silverware with a clunk and followed her into the bedroom.

"Mom, weren't you the one who taught me, 'Never take *anything* for granted?' "

4

Duffy, Up on the Hill

I was out in the back one afternoon, giving a pep talk to the seven surviving impatiens plants, when the telephone rang.

"Hello," I said, rushing in and answering it on the third ring.

"May I speak to Miss . . . Heather . . . Mallory, please."

The voice was measured and stiff, as if the caller were reading a message.

"This is me," I said.

"Miss Mallory, you have a dog named Tiger?"

"Yes . . ." I had a prickly feeling up the back of my neck. Suddenly I realized I hadn't seen Tiger in a while. Was this the police? Had he been hit by a car?

"What's the matter?" I asked. "Who *is* this?"

"It's me. Duffy, up on the hill," the voice answered.

It took a moment for me to make the connection. The old man!

"Your dog has been digging in my garden. I have him tied up here, and you'd better come and get him."

"Oh ... oh ... yes, I'll come right away!" I said, and I hung up. But then I just stood there, too stunned to move. How had Tiger gotten into the garden? And why did the old man have to tie him up? A clammy feeling swept over me. I didn't want to go up there alone. Why isn't anybody ever around when you need them? Lisa had left this morning, Marshall was off in his camper (though a lot of good he'd be even if he were home), and Mom, of course, was at the shop. Then I thought of tiny, defenseless Tiger, and I flew out the kitchen door. Tied up! Why did he have to tie him up just because he had dug in his precious garden? It was true what they said about him. He was just a rich old ... *mean* old man!

I ran all the way up the road, and by the time I got to the old man's property I could hardly breathe. People called it the Reynolds' estate because that was the name of the original owners. I don't know why everyone made such a fuss about it. It was just a big white house. But it was very old, maybe that's what made it so special. Some things are valuable when they get to be very old. That was it ... the Reynolds' house was an antique! As I started up the steps to the front door, I thought of the man I had seen in Brockmeyer's. How old had he been? Did people get to be antiques if they lived long enough?

There was a porch—I think it's what they call a veranda—encircling the house as far as the eye could see. There were two big double doors painted green, and on each one there was a large knocker in the shape of a lion's head. I stood up straight and pushed the hair out of my eyes. I was glad I was wearing my new T-shirt. He'd see that I wasn't just some scruffy little kid whose dog he could abuse. I took a deep breath and banged on the door with the knocker. It was tarnished and rusty and it made a dull *thud thud* sound.

I waited, but nothing happened, so I banged on the door again. Again the *thud thud* and then silence. I started walking along the porch until I came to the corner and peeked around. But all I saw was another long stretch of porch. There were trees towering over the house on each side, and I wondered where all this land was that everybody talked about.

I walked along the side of the house until I came to the other end. When I turned a corner, it was as if I had come out of a tunnel into the sunlight. The back of the property seemed to go on forever: a meadow filled with wild flowers rolling out as far as I could see. Over to one side there was a pond with a picket fence around it and a huge weeping willow tree. And there were more flowers all over the place, millions of them. It was the first real-life garden I had ever seen that looked better than the pictures in the garden catalogs. And in the middle of it all, sitting on a stone bench, holding my dog, was Thomas Worthington Duffy.

At the same moment that I spotted them, Tiger saw me and started to yelp and bark. But he didn't jump down and run to me. Then I noticed it—a white handkerchief was tied around his leg. Tiger was hurt!

I dashed down the steps of the porch and across the short stretch of lawn between us. I tried to scoop Tiger up in my arms, but he started to whimper.

"What happened?" I demanded.

"The little fellow decided to dig in my rose bushes this

afternoon," he said. "Got a thorn caught in his paw, and when he tried to get it out, he scratched himself some more in the brambles. I figured it was better to tie him up so he couldn't hurt himself anymore." He gestured to the white cloth bound around his paw. So that was what he meant when he said that he had Tiger "tied up."

"You didn't tell me he was hurt," I said.

The old man looked at me blankly for a moment. "Didn't I? Well, I intended to," he said. "Good thing he has this tag," he added, "so I knew who he belonged to."

I felt a little guilty then for being so suspicious, but I was still cautious as I sat down on the bench next to them. I made sure there was a good distance between the old man and me as I gathered Tiger into my arms.

"I'm sorry he dug up your garden," I said. "I try to keep him in, but he always ends up getting out and getting into trouble."

The old man looked at Tiger. "You didn't get into trouble, did you? You're just a dog, for mercy's sake. What does she expect you to do . . . sit in a chair, smoking a pipe and reading a newspaper?"

That made me laugh, and I could feel the knot inside me loosen as I sat petting Tiger and let the warm afternoon sun beat down on me. I looked around and there were beautiful things everywhere. The flowers were crowded together with no thought to what went where, so the effect was like those paintings I had seen in a museum once: blurry, with flowers and meadow and sky misting together into a kind of rainbow.

The old man turned and looked at me. "You look familiar."

"I met you one day in Brockmeyer's," I said.

"No you didn't. I haven't been in there for years."

"I'm sorry" I said, beginning to feel nervous again, "but you *were*. You told me to buy some impatiens. Don't you remember?"

He didn't say anything for a moment. Then he suddenly snapped back. "Ah yes, *now* I remember. How are they doing?"

"Some of them are doing okay. But some of them have died."

We sat in silence for a while, and I figured I'd better be getting home. But then he looked over at me and said. "What's that you've got on your shirt?"

"This is my gardening T-shirt. My grandmother sent it to me. See?" I looked down and pointed to the words on the front.

"Flower . . . Power . . ." he read slowly, looking so serious that for a moment I wanted to laugh. He sure was a strange old man. "Flower power," he repeated to himself. "What a lovely thought, uh, what was your name?"

"Heather. Heather Mallory."

"Heather. Excellent name for a gardener. Lovely flower, grows in Scotland. Did you know that?"

"Yes, I did."

"Does it have any magical powers?"

"Excuse me?"

"Does it have any magical powers?"

"My name?"

"No, no, your *T-shirt*."

He must have noticed the blank look on my face because he shook his head. "No, I guess not. I thought perhaps it was an *enchanted* T-shirt," he said with a sigh, "but you youngsters don't go in for that sort of thing anymore, do you?"

"What sort of thing?" I said, a bit impatiently. He wasn't making any sense.

"Enchantment, magical powers, make-believe."

"Oh . . . oh, no," I said quickly, beginning to understand. "You mean like fairy tales. No, I'm too old for that sort of thing."

"How old are you?"

"Eleven."

"That old, eh?" he said, shaking his head. "You certainly don't look it."

I could feel my face getting red. I hoped I hadn't made him mad. How old was he, I wondered?

Then he said, "Did you *ever* believe in that sort of thing, Heather Mallory?"

The question caught me by surprise, because, of course, it was true that I never did. But he couldn't know! I had always felt superior to kids who believed in things like the Tooth Fairy and the Easter Bunny. I shook my head.

"I didn't think so. That's a pity."

"No it isn't!" I said. "Make-believe can be a tremendous waste of time and an escape from reality." My mother had said that to me once when we were getting books out of the library. It must have burrowed into some corner of my memory just to come popping out now to embarrass me.

"And what's wrong with escaping from reality now and then, uh . . . what did you say your name was?"

"Heather . . ." I answered.

"Yes, yes, of course. You must excuse me. I know some things as neat as can be. But some days I can't remember my *own* name." He shook his head in that funny way I remembered from Brockmeyer's.

I knew then that Thomas Worthington Duffy wasn't really mean. He was just old and frail and living in a house that, like his clothes, was much too big for him.

I got up to go. He looked at me, and I noticed again how bright his eyes were in his ruddy, wrinkled face. They were the bluest eyes I'd ever seen.

"I guess you want to get going," he said.

"Yes. I have to get home. . . ." But suddenly I wanted to be nice to the old man. Hadn't he taken care of Tiger? And showed me what flowers to buy? It wouldn't hurt to humor him.

"Mr. Duffy," I said, "maybe I was wrong. Maybe this *is* an enchanted T-shirt. I mean, how should I know? If it is, what could it do?"

"What could it do? What a question to ask . . . what a question," he said. With all his muttering, I couldn't help feeling that he was pleased with me. "The proper thing to ask, Heather Mallory, is: If something is enchanted"—and at this his voice dropped to a whisper as if we were sharing a secret—"what *couldn't* it do?"

I found myself rooted to the spot. Even Tiger had stopped squirming in my arms. "All right," I whispered back, "what couldn't it do?"

"Nothing," he said, sitting back and looking pleased with himself. "There would be nothing in this world it couldn't do." His eyes looked at me steadily now, and he didn't look so old suddenly. "Except perhaps," he added, "make our friend here into much of a watchdog."

As if he knew he was being talked about, Tiger cocked his head to one side, and his tail started twirling like an airplane propeller.

"I really do have to go now, Mr. Duffy," I said.

"Just Duffy. That's what my friends always called me."

"Thank you for taking care of Tiger."

"You're very welcome. He's a lovely dog. Even Jezebel likes him," and he gestured to where a gray and white cat slept peacefully under the willow tree. "And please come again. Anytime. Next time I will cut you some flowers."

"That would be lovely."

"You can go around that way," he said, walking slowly with me to a path through the shrubbery at the side of the house.

I had just started down the path when I turned and looked back at him. "You were only fooling, right, Mr. Duffy? About this T-shirt being enchanted?"

He looked at me. "That's for you to decide, Heather Mallory," he said with a smile. "After all, it is your T-shirt."

I thought about that all the way home. I knew it was ridiculous, but it made me feel good.

5

Superdad

When I got home, Mom was there. I could tell right away she was in a bad mood. She had a pinched look around her eyes that she gets when she's had a bad day at the shop.

"How come you're home so early?" I asked.

"Because things were slow," she said, "and I had a headache, and Liz said, 'Why don't you knock off early? I'll close up,' and I said 'That's a fine idea! I'll go spend some time with my daughter!' So I came home . . . to an empty house and *no note*. Where were you?"

"Why should I leave a note? How should I know you were going to get home early?"

"Where *were* you?"

I let out an exaggerated sigh. I hate it when Mom acts like the FBI. "Did you notice anything in my arms as I came in?" I asked. Tiger came limping over to my mother.

"What happened?" she said, scooping him up and examining the bandaged paw.

"He was hurt, and I had to go get him," I said.

"Where was he?"

I cleared my throat. "Up at Duffy's."

"Up at *where?*" she asked, her eyes widening.

"You know, the old man."

I told her then, exactly what had happened. Except I left out the part about my T-shirt being enchanted. I figured she might not understand about that.

"Heather, I don't think it's such a good idea, you going up there. He's a strange old coot. Hasn't been out of that house for years."

"I saw him in Brockmeyer's in the spring."

"You did? Why didn't you tell me?"

"Well, I guess you weren't around to tell."

As soon as I said them, I wanted to take the words back. That's something that's really hard about conversation. You say something and then you think, Oh no, let me switch those words around, I didn't mean it like that! If you're writing a composition for school, you can do that; you can switch the words around. But once words are spoken, they're gone, and there's no way you can get them back. But I tried anyway.

"I didn't mean it that way," I said.

"Oh I know, I know," she said, flashing me a quick, tight smile. She took some lettuce out of the salad bin and started rinsing it under the faucet.

"I'll do that," I said.

"No, that's okay."

I sat at the kitchen table and watched my mother's back hunched over the sink. Maybe it wasn't just the shop. I

42

wondered suddenly if she felt bad about things changing over at the Benedicts. Mom pretends to think it's great that we're like sisters, but sometimes she gets real uptight about not being, well . . . like Lisa's mother. Mrs. Benedict and Mom used to sit right at this table drinking coffee and talking for hours at a time. They went to meetings together to hear people talk about the problems of the single parent. Now, I guess, she's lost someone, too.

On an impulse, I went over and gave her a hug.

"Egads, what's the occasion? It's not my birthday!"

"Maybe you don't need hugs once in a while, but I do," I said, laughing. But when I said it, I felt a twinge. Because I wasn't really joking.

I set the table, and for a few minutes we worked side by side in silence. Finally I said, "He's not so weird, Mom."

"Well, I'm sure he's harmless, Heather. It's just, well, people talk."

"Like about Halloween?"

"Oh, you've heard that one, huh?"

"Oh sure. But I didn't see any bats. In fact, his garden is beautiful."

"That used to be quite a showplace. It's a shame he's let the place get so run-down. Well, maybe when he goes, someone will take it over who'll fix it up nice again."

"*When he goes . . .*" She meant, when he *dies*. He's so old, it could happen any time now. I thought about him sitting on that stone bench, just waiting to die.

"You know, Mom, he's old *looking*, but I think his mind's real good. He's the one who told me to buy the impatiens

43

that day in Brockmeyer's. He seemed kind of cranky at first, but I think he really wants to be friendly. He's just out of practice."

"Well, even so, I don't think it's a good idea you going up there. You certainly don't need the company of somebody like him." She let out a deep sigh. "Let's eat early, I have a stack of trade journals to get through tonight."

We made some hamburgers and ate them outside. I had made iced tea and by the time we were finished eating, everything was fine again. I have to have things all right between us. Since we're the only ones here, I just can't stand it when they're not.

I got a postcard from Lisa. It had a picture of a dolphin jumping into the air and flapping his flippers. The little print on the back of the card said, GREETINGS FROM SEA KINGDOM AQUARIUM, RTE. 122, SPRINGDALE. *It's really great here,* she wrote. *We go swimming every day. No rain so far. See you soon, Love, Lisa.*

The same day I got the postcard from Lisa, I saw Marshall's camper parked in his driveway. But two days went by, and I didn't see any sign of Marshall. Then one morning he showed up at the back door just as I was finished stacking the dishwasher.

"When did you get home?" I asked, not letting on that I had noticed a two-ton trailer practically sitting in my living room.

"Couple of days ago. Boy, did we have a great time."

He helped himself to a cupcake and stretched out in one of the kitchen chairs as he talked. I was a little miffed that he was never around anymore, and the thought occurred to me that he had his nerve, just coming in and making himself at home like things hadn't changed.

"You've only been gone two weeks," I said.

"Boy, did we have a great time."

"Yeah, but you said you'd be gone for *three* weeks."

"Was it ever fun."

"Well, how come?" I asked, trying to keep my voice steady and not betray how annoyed I was feeling.

He looked at me through his horn-rims and sighed like I was the dumbest thing that had ever been born.

"That's what happens when you have a camper, dummy. It's not like you're staying at a motel where you have to check in and out. We wanted to stay longer, but Herb had to get back. But boy, was it neat," he said, enunciating the words slowly, in case I hadn't gotten the message yet. "We heard a bear one night, but Herb scared him off."

"You heard a real bear?" I said, not trying to hide the skepticism in my voice.

"No, a stuffed bear. A big fat teddy bear, dummy."

"Marshall, if you call me dummy one more time, I'm gonna sock you."

"What's the matter with you?"

"What's the matter with *me*? You come in here, bragging your head off about Su— about your stepfather, and stuffing your face with my cupcakes, and calling me dummy, and you ask what's the matter with me?"

"Yeah," he said.

I stood there for a moment while he stared at me in that owlish way of his, and then we both burst out laughing at the same time. It started as a fit of giggles, but soon we were *hurting,* we were laughing so hard.

"So what's happened around here while I was gone?"

I took a deep sigh. "Nothing, Marshall," I said truthfully. "Absolutely nothing. Oh, except that I'm taking an origami class in the summer workshop."

"Ori— what?"

"Origami. It's this way the Japanese have of folding paper. You make little birds and things. I've gone twice so far."

"Oh."

"And . . . I did go up to visit a neighbor of ours one day."

"Who?" he said, licking the icing off his fingers.

"Thomas Worthington Duffy," I said smugly. Since everyone in the neighborhood used to run the other way at the mere sound of his footsteps, I felt entitled to a little admiration . . . awe . . . *envy.*

What I got from Marshall was, "Who?"

"The *old man,*" I said.

"Oh. Why didn't you say so?"

"I did. That's his name."

"Yeah, but nobody ever calls him that."

"Marshall, did you hear what I said? I went up to see him. To the house . . . the *Halloween* house."

"What'd you do that for?"

"Because Tiger got up there and got hurt, and I had to rescue him," I said. This was not the breathless reaction I had expected. Obviously if it didn't happen in a camper, Marshall wasn't interested.

"Bet you were scared," he said.

"Well, a little. You would have been, too."

"Naw, I wouldn't have."

"Marshall, you're a big liar! You know none of the kids will go near that place, and I did and I was all alone!" *And I want a medal for it* I could have added.

"Well, what happened? You're making such a big thing about it. Does he really drool at the mouth like Frankie says? Did you see bats fly out of the toilets?"

"Well, I wasn't *inside* the house," I began, and then, just as it had that day with Lisa in Brockmeyer's, my conscience began to bother me. I suddenly felt terribly sorry for the old man. What must it be like to live where everybody thinks you're a monster?

"No, Marshall, he doesn't drool at the mouth. He's kind of grouchy, but he's kind of lonely, too. If you want to know the truth—he's just a regular person." I hesitated a moment. Should I add, Oh, except that he thought my T-shirt might be enchanted . . . ? No . . . just as I hadn't told my mother, I wouldn't tell Marshall. I decided to change the subject. "Tell me about the bear," I said.

Marshall didn't need coaxing. "Well," he began, "we were asleep, but Herb heard something, and he went outside to investigate. He's not afraid of anything, Herb isn't. I could hear this terrible growling and shouting—it woke me up—and then there was a lot of rustling when the bear ran away."

"When the bear *ran away?*"

"Yeah. If he hadn't, we'd all be dead by now."

"Marshall, that's the biggest fib I ever heard."

"It is not! You can ask my mom."

47

"You're telling me that a bear came to your camper, and old Herb went outside and yelled at it and it *ran away?*"

"Yeah."

"Did you see it?"

Marshall's face got red, so I knew I had him.

"I didn't have to see him. I could hear him."

"Oh, what did he say?" I lowered my voice to sound bearlike: "Hello there, I'm a bear and I haven't had supper yet. . . ."

"Very funny. If Herb said it was a bear, then it was a bear!"

"Did Herb actually *see* the bear?"

"I don't know!"

"What'd you mean, you don't know? Did he wrestle with it or not?"

"He knows the sounds a bear makes, and he said it was a bear that was running through the woods!"

"Oh, bear footsteps . . . get it, *bare* footsteps, like I make every morning when I get out of bed!"

Marshall looked like he was getting really mad, but I didn't care. I wasn't gonna let him sit there and tell a bunch of dumb lies.

"Are you calling Herb a liar?"

"Me? Call Superdad a liar? My goodness . . ."

But I didn't get a chance to finish whatever I was going to say. Marshall looked absolutely furious. He jumped out of the chair and bolted out the door. But not before he turned and hissed, "You're just jealous because I've got a father now, and yours is still dead! *And he always will be!*"

I stood there too stunned to speak. I guess I did get pretty

48

nasty. I shouldn't have called Herb "Superdad." But for Marsh to say that. . . . I felt hollow inside, like one of those chocolate rabbits you get at Easter.

Marshall's real father was alive somewhere, but they never saw him. He just walked out on them when Marshall was a baby. Mom always said that was worse than a father getting killed in a car accident like my dad. I mean, my dad would be here if he could. That was *something*.

I slumped into the kitchen chair and did a dumb thing. A dumb thing I almost never do anymore, and I'm almost ashamed to tell you about. I put my head down on the table and bawled like a baby.

6
Sparrow

The volcano nestled peacefully in the palm of Mrs. Sagano's hand. I nudged Mary Tyson, who was sitting next to me on the floor of the community center.

"I'm really not in a volcanic mood this morning," I said. "They're so *messy*."

Mary giggled. Mary and I used to play together when we were in Mrs. Taylor's class, back in second grade. Of all the kids in the origami workshop, she was the one I knew best, so I always sat next to her.

I flipped through the workbook that Mrs. Sagano had handed out on the first day. I'd already made a hut and a wigwam. Maybe today I could make something graceful, like a bird. Here was one, a peacock. And there was a robin and a sparrow. The sparrow looked the easiest. I raised my hand.

"Yes . . . Heather, isn't it?"

I nodded. "Could I make a sparrow instead of a volcano?"

Mrs. Sagano hesitated. "That might be more difficult. How many steps is it?"

"Only seven. The volcano's five."

She nodded. "All right, go ahead and try it." She smiled at me.

I got into a comfortable position and read the directions intently. It didn't look too hard. The others were already halfway through their volcanoes. One girl's was almost ready to erupt.

I worked as fast as I could, but by the time the class was over I still wasn't finished.

"Do you want to stay here and finish, or do you want to take it home?" Mrs. Sagano asked.

Mary was ready to go, but she said, "I'll stay with you if you want. You're almost done."

"Thanks," I said.

Mary walked around looking at the trophies in the glass cases while I carefully folded the last feather on my sparrow. It was very simple, but since a sparrow is so small and delicate, you have to be very careful. I could hear the *click click* of a typewriter from one of the offices in the other part of the center. When I had finished, I stood up, holding my masterpiece at arm's length.

"That's very pretty," Mary said.

I wrinkled my nose to show her how unimpressed I was with my handiwork. I had made it with a blue piece of paper. I know sparrows aren't blue, but it was prettier this way.

"That's what I should have made," Mary said, holding a mud-colored volcano limply by her side.

"Next week, why don't you?"

"I think I will."

"Wait'll the teacher finds out that next time I'm making a bird in a nest. I saw it in the book. It's thirteen steps."

"Why do you like to do the tough ones?" she asked as we walked out the door together.

"Because it's not as boring when it's hard," I said. Mary had her bicycle, and I waved good-bye as I started to walk. "Thanks for waiting with me. See you Friday."

It was a fifteen-minute walk home, and I played with my sparrow as I went along. I decided to name him Stanley. That was a good name, Stanley Sparrow. I felt better than I had in days. All it took was this small, silly-looking paper bird. I was getting weird, definitely weird.

As I headed up Lehigh, I got *more* weird. I suddenly wanted to go see Mr. Duffy's garden again. I knew Mom wouldn't like it, but I figured if I'm on my own, I'm on my own. I'm supposed to be so grown-up I don't need anybody to hang around and take me places, or pay attention to me, or even talk to me. But my mom thinks she can still make rules like I'm a little kid. No way. It's not fair.

I hurried past our driveway. It was like making a sparrow when everybody was making volcanoes. I wanted to be different. I *was* different. . . .

As I climbed the stairs, I rehearsed what I would say: "Good afternoon, Mr. Duffy. I came to say thank you for saving my dog's life." No good. I'd already thanked him. And besides, he hadn't really saved Tiger's life. And I should call him Duffy, just Duffy. Sounds disrespectful for an old person, but he asked me to. What had he said . . . ? "That's what my friends always called me." It sounded like he didn't have any friends left. Had they all died? Or had he just lost touch with them because he was a recluse? Did he mean that I was his friend now, or that he wanted me to be?

When I got to the top, I walked around the veranda without knocking on the doors, and sure enough, there he was in the garden. But he wasn't sitting on the bench like before. He was kneeling amidst a row of white flowers, digging and pulling weeds out of the earth.

I went down the steps and it came over me slowly, almost as if I were being enveloped in a fog: the feeling that the scene in front of me was too beautiful to be real. It was a picture, a painting, a page from a book. But the garden was real. I knew it as soon as I got near enough to hear the bees buzzing and the chirping of birds in the trees overhead. I noticed a rose trellis that I hadn't seen before and Jezebel dozing on a moss-covered rock near the weeping willow. The sea of wild flowers seemed to be waving to me from the meadow.

I wondered whether to call to him or not. I didn't want to come up behind him and startle him. But as I approached, he looked up and he didn't seem at all surprised to see me. He just seemed pleased.

"Hello there," he said.

"Hi, Mr. Duffy."

He stared at me.

"Duffy," I corrected myself. "I intended to remember."

He grumbled something and went back to his work. I sat down on the bench and watched him. His grumbling didn't frighten me anymore, I realized. He reminded me of one of the kids in my class who always got mean when things didn't go the way he wanted. There was a mosquito buzzing nearby, but that was the only sound. The garden was perfectly still. It was that kind of summer day when even the flowers seem to be sleepy. I had this terrific feeling of contentment, of joy almost. Flowers always make me feel good, but this garden was special.

Finally he got up and wiped his forehead with a gloved hand. His battered old hat was pushed back from his face.

"What's that?" he asked, nodding to the sparrow that lay quietly in my lap.

I held it up. "It's a paper sparrow. I made it in origami class."

"Origami. Ah yes, lovely."

"You know what it is?"

"Yes, I know. The Japanese are a very creative people. Have you ever seen a bonsai garden?"

I shook my head.

He came over and sat down next to me on the bench. "The Japanese grow these trees, which, by very careful cultivation, remain very small. Dwarf, they're called."

"How do you know about these, whatever you called them?"

"*Bonsai* trees. If you live long enough, Heather, you can learn about a lot of things! I see you're wearing your Flower

Power T-shirt." He said the words *Flower Power* very slowly and exactly, making them seem very important.

"It's my favorite. Did I tell you my grandmother sent it to me from Chicago?"

He shook his head. "I don't remember if you did or not. You see, Heather, my head's just packed with all these ideas I've collected over the years. It's kind of like a house with too much furniture. I misplace things. If I'm going to have room for origami or bonsai, I have to put where-you-got-your-T-shirt up in the attic out of the way. I guess I should apologize."

"That's okay."

"So your grandmother lives in Chicago?"

"Yep. She's a buyer for one of the big department stores."

"Oh, that sounds like an important job. Do you see her often?"

"Not really. She was going to visit us this summer, but she's too busy. Maybe in the fall she'll come."

"And what does your father do?"

I swallowed hard. It seemed strange that Duffy didn't know anything at all about me when we had lived on the same street for so long. "I don't have a father anymore," I said. "He died when I was little."

"I'm terribly sorry."

"That's okay. He was killed in a car accident."

"Do you have any brothers or sisters?"

"Nope. Just me and Mom. Mom owns The Treasure Chest, you know, the gift shop in town?"

He looked vague, and I realized he probably never went

into town. I knew he had his food delivered; I'd seen the truck from Sam's Market going up the hill lots of times.

"Duffy," I said, getting used to calling him that, "do you do this all yourself?"

"The garden, you mean?"

I nodded.

"Mostly. I have a man comes in and cuts the grass. Gets rid of a tree or two when needed. But the flowers I take care of myself. Why, they're more like my friends than just things that grow out of the ground. But it gets smaller and smaller every year. Can't keep it up the way I used to."

I couldn't help thinking how much younger he seemed today. His speech was clearer, his movements quicker. As he spoke, I looked over at a mass of purple irises, golden snapdragons, phlox and bluebells. I knew the names of all the flowers from reading my garden catalogs. There were giant red poppies near the pond, and a mass of lilies of the valley spread out at my feet. I looked up at him. "Could I help?" I asked.

"What?"

"Could I help you? With the flowers, I mean. If you show me what to do, I'm sure I wouldn't kill any of them."

"No, no, that's very kind of you, but I don't need any help, really."

I was disappointed. "Okay," I said. Maybe he *did* like being alone all the time, after all. Maybe I was intruding. "I guess I'd better go now," I said.

But when I stood up, he stood up, too.

"Would you like a cold drink?" he asked, and without waiting for an answer, he went up to the house.

I waited for a moment, and then I followed him through the open back door. A musty, stale smell greeted me. Duffy's kitchen was very neat, but it had a strange, empty feeling about it. The walls were a dingy white, and the old-fashioned appliances were the same color. In the corner there was a small table with one lonely chair tucked neatly under it. I'm used to kitchens that are busy and bright; this one was spooky, like a ghost kitchen that nobody ever really cooked or ate in.

He ran the water in the sink until it got cold and then took two glasses from a cabinet over the sink. I shook my head when he held up a glass. "I'm not thirsty," I said.

While he drank the water, I glanced beyond the kitchen into the living room, where there were velvet chairs and drapes tied with long satin tassels and, on the walls, paintings in fancy gold frames. It was a very formal living room, almost like you'd see in a palace. Except that everything was covered with dust.

Duffy stood looking out the window for a moment. "I used to have a lot of friends, Heather. But, well, for one reason or another . . . heck, I've outlived most of them!" he said, laughing as if it were a good joke. "Would you really like to work in my garden?"

"Yes, I would," I said.

"Then I'd be glad to have you. Would be like having Billy around again."

I wanted to ask him who Billy was, but he was out the door, marching back toward the meadow. The more I got to know him, the younger he seemed. I was beginning to think it was just the *outside* of him that was old.

"When should I come back?" I yelled.

"Whenever you like! But I warn you, I just might make a gardener out of you!"

I waved good-bye then and was halfway down the street when I realized I had forgotten Stanley. He must have fallen out of my lap when I followed Duffy into the house. I wondered for a moment whether to go back; it was only a paper bird, but if the cat got at it, or it rained, it would be gone forever.

I mounted the steps and came around the porch once more, but at the back steps I stopped. I needn't have worried about my sparrow. Duffy was fixing him to a branch of the weeping willow tree, where he could look down on the garden while we worked. It was a fine place for a sparrow. I couldn't have given him any better.

I turned and went home.

7

Emily Leonard's Birthday Party

Twelve seems wonderfully old to me. I won't be twelve until November, and I can't wait. Emily Leonard was twelve on July 14, and there were six of us helping her celebrate. First, we were meeting at her house, where she would open her presents and we'd have a supper of hot dogs, potato chips, and birthday cake. Then, after dark, we were going to the amusement park over in Liddonsville.

Emily had just had her ears pierced, so I bought her a pair of yellow earrings. They were shaped like bananas. The store had peach earrings, and apple ones, too, but I thought the bananas were the prettiest.

We sat around on thick green carpeting in the Leonards' playroom while she opened the presents. (I noticed there were several boxes the same size as mine, and I wondered how many people had given Emily earrings.) The first box she opened was from Stephanie Packard, her best friend, who gave her a pair of tortoiseshell hair combs. Stephanie bought them when she was away at the beach, and they were shaped like seashells. Everybody made a big fuss and passed them around. I would love to be able to use hair combs. I wear my hair real short, and it's nice and wavy so it doesn't look too bad, but I'd love to have long hair like Lisa or Emily. But Mom's right when she says it's more practical this way. I'm not the type to fuss; some mornings I just comb it with my fingers.

"Now, which one should I open next?" Emily asked coyly. "Eeny-meeny-miney-moe." She picked up another small box and read the card slowly, *To Emily, Love always, your friend Cathy Mercer*. Personally, when I'm twelve, I'm going to act more mature. At the rate we were going, we'd never make it to the hot dogs, never mind the rides. And I was getting hungry. She undid the wrappings and held up a pair of little gold butterfly earrings. Cathy looked very smug when everybody oohed and aahed as they were passed around. Cathy is very pretty and very popular, but I don't really like her very much. In fact, if I didn't know it was wrong to hate someone, I could do a real good job of hating Cathy. She's so *mean*.

For instance, the next present Emily opened was another pair of earrings. They were little gold turtles from Mary Tyson, and you know what Cathy said? "I could have gotten you those, but I thought you'd like butterflies better than turtles."

When the box was passed to me, I said, "Oh, they're so cute! If I had pierced ears, I'd love a pair like these." Mary looked over at me and smiled. I think she knew why I was falling all over myself. I mean, they were cute turtles, but how cute can a turtle be?

When Emily finally opened my present, it was the next to last, and I was afraid she'd be getting tired of getting earrings. But she squealed, "Ooh, they're *darling!*" as if she really meant it. When she passed the box around, Cathy made a face and passed it on without hardly looking at them, but that's Cathy for you.

When we were finally on our way to Liddonsville, I realized I was having a good time, and I thought about all the fun I'd have telling Lisa about it when she got back. Maybe she'd even be jealous. Let's face it, you can't go off to a farm for the whole month of July and still go to Emily Leonard's birthday party. Nobody could, not even Lisa. That's just the way life is.

Emily had gotten a cute terry cloth jumpsuit for her birthday and as we got out of the car, I noticed her smoothing it down and tightening the belt. Emily's beginning to get a figure, and the boys were always staring at her. Of course, she's twelve now and I'm still only eleven, so I'm not really worried yet. But if nothing's started by November, I'm going to start worrying.

Since Stephanie is Emily's best friend, I knew that they would pair off, and Joan Engelhardt teamed with Cathy Mercer, so I doubled up with Mary.

You could hear the sounds of the amusement park even before we got out of the car. Mrs. Leonard left us at the front gate and told us she'd pick us up at the same spot at ten thirty. I love amusement parks at night, when the lights make everything dazzle. The Ferris wheel was twirling around in the sky like a toddler's toy, and the shrieks of kids on the roller coaster could be heard over the music from the merry-go-round.

"What do you want to go on first?" Emily asked. She had a thick book of tickets in her hand, enough to keep the six of us going for hours.

"How about the Caterpillar?" Joan said.

So we went on the Caterpillar first. That was fun, but pretty tame, and so were the next couple of rides we went on. Then Stephanie yelled, "There's the Rocket Ride!" and we all headed toward it. The Rocket Ride is a giant white roller coaster, and I noticed Mary didn't seem too happy about the idea. Mary's very fragile looking. I mean, she's so skinny she looks like Olive Oyl, and I think she was afraid—one good wind and—*Did you hear about Mary? She was last seen blowing west over Chicago. . . .*

She tried to be a good sport, but from the way she sat next to me with her eyes tightly shut, I could tell she was really scared. I wasn't all that brave myself. Every time the car reached the top and poised for a split second before it plunged downhill, my heart was in my mouth. By the time we had rolled to a stop, I was hoarse from screaming, and I noticed Mary's face had a green tinge.

"Don't tell me you were *scared?*" Cathy said, not trying to hide the disgust in her voice.

"I wasn't scared," Mary said.

"Of course she wasn't," Emily added.

But from the way Mary had said it, with her voice shaking, it was obvious she was. So right away Cathy said, "Let's go on the parachute jump."

I saw Mary's green face turn white. "Why don't we take it easy for a minute," I said. "I don't want to throw up all over the place."

"Well, aren't you the charming one," Cathy said, rolling her eyes in a way that made everyone giggle.

"Why don't we just go on the Ferris wheel?" Emily said. "That'll give us a rest." So since she was the birthday girl, that's what we did.

I suddenly realized I wasn't the only one who didn't like Cathy Mercer. She seemed to really bug Emily. Maybe Cathy was taking Lisa's place, not me!

From the top of the Ferris wheel, we could see clear to Fairview. I knew it was Fairview because they have a big hotel there that has a tower that lights up at night. The park spread out beneath us in a circle of wildly spinning lights as Mary and I played a game: trying to spot people we knew on the ground. For a moment I thought I saw Marshall, but then I decided the boy was too short. But he did *look* like Marshall, and it hurt me to look at him so I turned away. We could never, ever be friends again, I knew that, and it hurt so bad. It was as if he had died.

There was a new attraction at the park this summer called the Monster Maze. The ads promised that you would either (1) faint, (2) have a heart attack, (3) throw up, or (4) all three, if you went on it. Naturally, that turned out to have the longest line of all.

"Let's get some cotton candy before we get on line,"

Emily suggested, and of course we all agreed and lined up at the cotton candy booth. I was next to last on line, and when I finally got mine, I took a big bite and I thought I'd never breathe again. I had sticky pink "cotton" on my nose, in my eyes, and on my cheeks. I must have looked pretty silly, because I could hear Mary laughing. I turned to tell her to stop it, and then I saw something that made me almost choke.

This time he wasn't too short. This time he didn't just look like Marshall. The two of them, Marshall and Ricky, were standing at the shooting gallery next door. Marshall had the rifle up on his shoulder, and I could hear the *rat-tat-tat* over the general din of the carnival. Behind the two of them, standing with his hands in his pockets but shouting directions, was Superdad.

My throat felt dry. Mary came over and said, "Let's try the penny arcade, okay?"

"Uh, sure," I said. I might as well. I could stand here all night, and even if he turned and saw me, he would probably look away. And if he didn't, if he came over and said "Hi!" like nothing had happened, what would I do? Would *I* turn and walk away? *You're just jealous because I've got a father now and yours is still dead. And he always will be!* For a horrible instant I could feel my eyes fill up, and I thought I was going to start crying again. There must be some kind of virus going around this summer. I never cry. Crying is for babies.

"Let's go," I said to Mary. But as I said it, I heard a squeal from Emily.

"Look, it's Ricky and Marshmallow!" she said. "Come on, let's go over."

Mary started to follow them, but I pulled her back. "What's the matter?" she said.

"I thought you wanted to go to the penny arcade."

"We can go in a minute. I wanna listen. You know Emily likes Ricky."

I trailed behind as she joined Stephanie and Emily just as Marshmallow put the chained rifle back on the counter. Superdad was gesturing, holding an imaginary rifle to his shoulder, showing Marshall what he had done wrong. *Good.* When they saw the girls, I noticed Marsh's face turning red. That meant he was embarrassed by whatever Superdad was saying. *Double good.*

Then he looked beyond them and saw me, but he quickly turned away.

"Have you guys been to the Monster Maze yet?" Ricky asked, looking directly at me.

"Uh-uh," I said, my mouth filled with cotton candy. "Have you?"

"Yep. It was neat. I almost threw up," Marshall answered.

I didn't look at him. I heard Superdad say, "That's because you ate too much junk. I told you you'd feel sick."

"Are you going to try it?" Marsh persisted.

I could feel the knot in my stomach easing a little, but all I could manage in reply was "I guess so."

"Let's go on it now! It's getting late, and my mother will be coming to pick us up," Emily said.

"Yeah. Let's take our cotton candy on it and see who pukes first," Cathy said, looking over at me. I saw Emily making a face in Cathy's direction.

We said good-bye and started over to the giant green

monster "mouth" that served as the entrance. There was a long line, and as we got on the end of it, I heard Ricky yell at Emily,

"Maybe they'll go easy on you if you tell them it's your birthday, Em."

Emily blushed and yelled, "Stop it!" But you could tell she was pleased. Just having Ricky Schneider notice her was probably the best birthday present of all. I don't think Ricky's so cute, but most of the girls do.

I noticed Mary quickly finishing her cotton candy and throwing the stick away. I did the same. Why ask for trouble?

As we neared the entrance and our turn to get into the seats that would propel us through the Monster Maze, I gave one quick look back to where we had left Ricky and Marshall. But there was no one there but a fat lady and her two fat children; they were arguing over the last bite of a hot dog.

Everybody started squealing as soon as the seats started to move. Mary grabbed my arm so tightly I thought she would draw blood.

"Take it easy," I said. "We haven't even started yet."

As our seats slid into the black tunnel, I could feel every muscle in my body stiffen. But there was only silence. Silence and blackness. I could hear Mary breathing next to me, and behind me, the barely audible giggles of the other girls.

Then I felt it. At first I thought I was imagining things, but it continued to curl itself around my ankle: something cold and slimy, slithering, crawling. . . . Then I heard the scream, loud and clear, piercing the chill, damp air. It was a split second before I realized that I was the one who had screamed. At the same instant, the "snake" stopped crawling around my ankle, but now Emily was shrieking, and Mary, with one arm still locked through mine, was trying to get out of the seat.

"Sit down," I said, still trembling, but now more out of embarrassment than fear. How had they done that? It felt just like a snake. And was I the only one? Or was that what Emily had been screaming about? An eerie light came on, and I glanced down at my lap. My hands were the hands of a ninety-year-old woman. I turned to Mary, and we both let out a yelp at the same time. Mary looked old, withered, and cronelike, and from the horror on her face, I could tell I looked the same. Darkness again. Then a scream, and the unmistakable sounds of someone being stabbed to death. Then a light spraying, as if I had been standing too close and some of the blood had spurted on me. A picture flashed just ahead. It was too fast to be made out quickly, but it was someone being chopped up. I began to feel sick. Then a sudden turn, and we plunged downward, steep and fast, and just as we were about to topple out of our seats, we straightened out again and sped straight into ... a speeding car. I was screaming as loudly as everybody else now, everything coming at me too fast. It went on like this for a few more minutes, and then suddenly we were plunged back outside, all of us breathless and laughing and panting at the same time.

We stumbled out of our seats and Emily looked at her watch. "It's almost ten thirty. We've got to meet my mother at the gate. Come on."

Mary and I walked together. "Maybe you can come over to my house some day next week," she said. "I'll call you and my mom can pick you up. Come for lunch, okay?"

"Sure," I said.

We reached the entrance just as the big maroon station wagon pulled up. But we couldn't leave immediately. There was a slight delay while Cathy Mercer got sick in the rhododendron bushes at the side of the road.

I think that was the best birthday present Emily Leonard could have gotten.

8
The Funny Farm

Sometimes I think everybody in Oakfield has a station wagon except us. Not that I'm complaining. I agree with Mom: She drives a cute red compact car and refers to wagons as "trucks." But I guess if you've got a big family, a wagon makes sense. The one Mrs. Tyson picked me up in was bright green, and from the way it smelled inside I could tell it was new. There was a little girl in the back seat, snuggled up next to Mary. When I got in, she hid her face in Mary's lap.

"Kimberly, this is Heather. Say hello to Heather, Kim."

Kimberly looked up at me, stuck her tongue out, and dove back into Mary's lap.

"She's shy," Mary said.

I wasn't sure that was her problem, but I didn't say so to Mary. "I remember her," I said. "Wasn't she just a baby a few years ago?"

As soon as I said it, I realized how bright I sounded. Mary did, too, and we both laughed.

"That's right, you came over a couple of times when we were in Mrs. Taylor's class. She was about six months old then."

As we ignored her, Kimberly came out of hiding and offered me a stuffed animal she had been holding. It was either a bear or a dog; I couldn't be sure which, because it looked like it had led a hard life. The fur was threadbare, the ears were worn down to stubs, and the tongue and one eye were missing. I went to take it from her, but she snatched it back.

"Mine," she screeched.

"Okay, okay, you can keep the teddy bear," I said.

"Whirl!" she corrected me.

"*Whirl?*" I repeated, looking at Mary for guidance.

"She means squirrel," Mary said patiently. "She's correcting you because you called it a teddy bear."

"Oh . . ." I said. Kimberly was rubbing her eyes and staring at me petulantly.

"When we get to the house, she'll go in for an n-a-p," Mary said, spelling out the last word. "That's why she's so cranky," she added in a whisper.

What a nice big sister Mary was, I thought. Maybe I'd be that way, too, if I were in her position. But I have a feeling I'd give the kid a good whack. As I was thinking these serene thoughts, we pulled into the Tyson driveway. I remembered the house from a few years ago. It was a big sprawling contemporary with lots of glass.

Mrs. Tyson was a thin woman with quick, birdlike movements. She had been silent on the ride over, but as we got out of the car she gave me a tight smile and said, "I hope you two have a nice afternoon. You tell Ellie what you want for lunch, Mary. I'll see you later."

"Okay. Is Bobby going to be around?" Mary asked.

"I don't know, dear. But he won't bother you. I've got to run." She gave Kimberly a kiss on the cheek before she got into the car again and backed out of the driveway.

"Wanna go with Mommy . . ." Kimberly said, her lower lip beginning to quiver.

Mary picked her up and carried her into the kitchen.

"Ellie, this is Heather Mallory."

A stocky, middle-aged lady was working at the sink, and she nodded pleasantly to me as we came in.

"Let me put her down," Mary said, motioning to me to follow. I tried to stay at a safe distance, since Kimberly was glaring at me over Mary's shoulder.

Everything I saw as I passed through the house seemed to be either white or off-white and have chrome legs. While Mary took care of Kimberly, I waited in a small paneled room with leather chairs, a desk, and a television. I figured it must be her father's den, since the walls were covered with degrees her father had earned and pictures of her father with other men holding awards. There was even a picture of him catching a big fish. I noticed there weren't any pictures of *Mrs.* Tyson doing anything.

Mary came in and breathed a deep sigh of relief. "Whew, I'm glad that's over. She can be a real pain sometimes."

"Oh, but she's *cute*," I lied.

"Well, sometimes she is. Anyway, it's nice of you to say that. What do you want for lunch?"

71

I shrugged my shoulders. "I don't care," I said.

She marched ahead of me into the shiny kitchen and said, "Ellie, what do we have for lunch?"

"How about ham and cheese?" she said.

Mary turned and looked at me quizzically. "Okay?"

"Sure," I said.

We took our sandwiches and two glasses of lemonade out on the deck that overlooked their backyard. Actually, there wasn't any backyard. The Tysons' house was built right smack against the side of a hill, and when we sat on the deck, we could almost reach out and touch these big granite boulders.

"Your brother Bobby's in fourth grade, right?" I said.

"Yep. A real creep."

I giggled. "All boys are real creeps." Mary nodded her head in agreement as she munched on her sandwich. Looking around, I said, "Your house is so *big*."

Mary finished her sandwich and took a swallow of her lemonade. "When we built it, my grandmother was living with us, so we needed more room."

"I remember her! Doesn't she live with you anymore?"

Mary shook her head. Then she said, "Oh, look at that butterfly. Isn't it *beautiful*?"

A lovely orange and gold butterfly fluttered over the table, then flew up and away into a nearby clump of bushes. I looked around the back, and I noticed there weren't any flowers. Not one. The ground was covered with shrubs and hedges and little trees. I sank back in my chair and felt the sun on my face. That reminded me of Duffy's garden, and I sat there for a moment thinking how much prettier his place was. "Where does your grandmother live now?" I asked, pulling myself back to the present.

"The funny farm," a voice from behind me answered. I jumped around and stared at Bobby Tyson, who had climbed over the deck railing and stood two feet behind my chair.

"The *what?*"

"The funny farm," he repeated. "You know, the nuthouse."

"Bobby, stop it! If I told Mom what you said . . ."

"But you won't. You're too chicken!" he said as he opened the sliding glass door and went into the house.

"What did he mean?" I asked.

"Nothing," Mary said. But I could tell she was upset, and for some dumb reason, I felt responsible.

"I'm sorry," I said.

"It's not your fault. It's just Bobby. I wish he'd just . . . disappear. I *hate* him."

I didn't say anything. I didn't have any experience fighting with a brother or a sister. But I knew what it was like to hate somebody. That's the way I had been feeling about Marshall.

Finally Mary broke the silence. "If you must know, my grandmother's in Cedar Crest . . . the *nursing home.*"

"Well, what's so bad about that? Lots of old people live in nursing homes. Why did Bobby say what he did?"

"Oh, he thinks he's very clever. My mom would murder him. You see, Heather," she said, looking uncomfortable, "my grandmother is *senile.*"

"She's what?"

"Don't you know what senility is?" she asked. "It's something that happens to old people sometimes. They . . . they don't act right."

"Oh, that's awful," I said.

"Yeah, it is. She used to be so nice. She had that room next to Kimberly's. Up until just before Kim was born, she was a regular grandmother. Then she started forgetting things, things like where we lived, and sometimes she didn't even recognize people. One time she thought my dad was my grandfather . . . her *husband.* Can you imagine? Listen, I don't want to talk about it anymore, okay?"

"Sure, sure, Mary," I said.

But she continued. "I don't know why my mother keeps going to see her. That's where she went today. I mean, she doesn't even recognize her own daughter! Mom always looks like she's been crying when she gets back." We were silent for a moment, then all at once she said, "Come on, let's go exploring!"

"Great," I said.

We jumped down off the deck and started to scramble up the cliff at the back of the Tysons' house. It wasn't too hard to do, because there were small trees to hold on to. They clung to the side of the hill, some with their roots exposed, as if they had just barely escaped the bulldozer. When we got to the top, there was jungle as far as the eye could see. Mary went straight ahead, and I followed.

"How do you know where you're going?" I yelled.

She turned and gave me a self-satisfied grin, which made me feel better, because I still thought I was responsible for her getting upset.

"I live here, remember?" she said. Then, pointing first in one direction and then the other, she said, "Liddonsville is over there, and Cardigan Corners is over that way. Come on, there's a stream down here that's neat." I had to hustle to keep up with her because, of course, she knew the way and I kept tripping over things. Twice I got branches caught in my hair, and I had to stop to untangle myself. "Here it is!" she said. I could hear the gurgle of water, and then I saw a small, rushing stream tumbling over some rocks. It looked like Niagara Falls to someone who was sweating as much as I was. "Let's put our feet in," she said, and we did. But it was ice cold, so cold that I quickly pulled my toes out.

"Where does this come from?" I asked. "The North Pole?" We sat on the edge of the stream then, neither of us talking much, and it was very nice and peaceful. There were tiny white flowers growing along the bank, and Mary began to pick them. She made them into bracelets by tying their stems together. She made one for herself, and then she made one for me. "That's pretty," I said, slipping it over my wrist.

"That's *dumb*," she said, suddenly embarrassed.

"No it's not," I said, and I started to pick some myself. But I gathered mine into bunches. I could put them in juice glasses when I got home.

"I love flowers, don't you?" she said.

I nodded. "There's a house near me, it's sort of like a mansion . . . but not a fancy one, if you know what I mean, and the man who lives there has the most beautiful flowers I've ever seen. He talks to them and treats them almost like *people*. He says they're his friends."

75

"He sounds like my grandmother," Mary said. "Heather, do me a favor?"

"Sure," I said. "What is it?"

"Please don't tell anyone what I told you. I mean, they know my grandmother's in Cedar Crest, but I never say why."

"Well, sure, I mean, who would I tell? But Mary, I don't think it's anything to be ashamed of."

"You wouldn't understand," she said. "If you've never had a grandmother, you wouldn't understand."

"I have a grandmother," I said.

"Yeah, but you don't see her a lot. I mean, she doesn't live with you. I . . . I just don't want to talk about it, okay?"

I wondered why someone who didn't want to talk about something kept talking about it. But I didn't say anything.

After a while we made our way back to the house, and at four o'clock Mrs. Tyson came home. She looked as if she had been crying, just as Mary had predicted, but she gave me another of her quick, tight smiles, like a rubber band being stretched too wide.

When she drove me home, I said, "Thank you very much," to Mrs. Tyson, and told Mary how much fun it had been. And it was the truth. I had really enjoyed the afternoon.

After the car drove off, I lingered for a moment in front of my house. The late afternoon sun was filtering through the trees, and it was so pretty I just stood there admiring it. I had never really noticed the gnarled old oak tree that stood guard just a few feet from our driveway. Being quiet like this, I could even hear the soft bubbling of the stream that ran through a neighbor's woods. Then, as I turned, I saw a lone figure at the end of the road. Duffy was just starting up the path to his house. A few minutes sooner, and maybe he would have been passing by and I could have said "Hi!"

I thought about Mary's grandmother. What if I told Mary that my friend, the old man, thinks my T-shirt is enchanted? No, Thomas Worthington Duffy wasn't senile. He was just ... *eccentric*. That was the word. But I shuddered a little in the hot summer sunlight before I turned and went into the house.

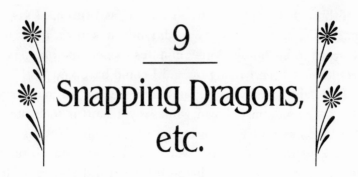

9
Snapping Dragons, etc.

"What kind of a name is Jezebel?" I asked. The cat had leaped up on my lap and sat with me under the weeping willow tree, purring.

Duffy smiled over at me. "By gosh, Heather, I had forgotten about that. Ruth named her. Ruth's favorite actress was Bette Davis, and she was in this movie about a Southern belle named *Jezebel*. Oh, you should have seen the goings-on in that movie! She was a regular . . . Well anyhow, this was way before you were born, probably when your mother was a little girl. Yep, 'cause our Billy was growing up then. Anyway, it was Ruth's favorite movie, and when we got a cat she named it Jezebel. When that one died, she named the next one Jezebel, too. And so on. Every cat we've had's been a Jezebel."

"Who's Billy?" I asked, stroking Jezebel as we talked. This was the second time he had mentioned him.

He looked at me for a second as if I had asked the dumbest

question in the world. "Billy? Of course you wouldn't know about Billy. How could you. Just a minute," he said, and hurried into the house. He returned in a few minutes with a framed picture of a young man in a soldier's uniform. It was a little faded, and it had that brown look that pictures get when they're getting old.

"This is Billy," he said quietly. "This was taken just before he went overseas."

"He . . . looks very nice," I said awkwardly. "Is he your son?"

"Yep. Mine and Ruth's. Only child we had."

"Where is he now?" I asked. But as soon as the words were out, I felt a chill sweep through me. Somehow I knew where he was, and I wanted desperately to take back the question.

"Gone," he said simply. "Killed in Korea. He was a hero, and only twenty-one years old."

"I'm sorry," I said.

"There's something very strange about life, Heather. Here I am, an old man, and whether I'm here or gone by my next birthday it doesn't matter a bit, to me or anybody else. But a boy like Billy, young and full of life . . ."

I had resumed working as we spoke, and the little trenches I was digging got deeper and deeper as the meaning of Duffy's words washed over me. Did he mean that he didn't care whether he lived or not? How awful it must be to be old!

"My father was twenty-eight when he was killed. I guess that's pretty young, too, isn't it?"

"That's pitiful young, Heather." I must have let out a sigh because he said, "You don't have to do anymore. I can finish."

"No, that's okay, I want to." I sifted the dirt and removed the three or four stones I found there. "I don't even remember my father," I said abruptly.

"How old were you when he died?"

"Three. Three years and two months. My birthday is in November, and he was killed in January. It was very icy . . . that's what caused the accident." Duffy didn't say anything, but he made little grunting noises that let me know he was listening. "Sometimes it bothers me that I can't remember him. I look at his picture and try and try, but it's no use."

"My goodness, you weren't more than a baby when he passed away. You can't feel bad about that, Heather."

"I know," I said, sitting back on my heels for a moment. I had never talked this way about my dad. Not to Lisa, that's for sure. Once, when I first met Lisa, she told me that I was the first friend she ever had whose father had died. She had lots of friends whose parents were divorced, but none of them had a father who was dead. She made it seem like he had done something terrible. I remember I went home that day and cried, and ever since then I just don't talk about my dad at all.

Duffy took his hat off, and I noticed for the first time that the top of his head was completely bald. He looked like one of Santa's elves.

"It's awfully hot now, isn't it?" he said. "What's the time?"

I looked at my watch. "It's three o'clock," I said.

"We'll stop now. I don't want you working too hard. Are you sure your mother doesn't mind you coming up here?"

I shook my head. "Of course not," I said. I was glad my face was flushed from the heat, so he couldn't tell that I was blushing. Mom didn't ask me much about how I spent my days, because she was doing inventory at the store, so I just hadn't told her. Anyway, she hadn't forbidden me to see Duffy. She had just said she didn't think it was a good idea.

"Let me cut you some snapdragons before you go."

"You don't have to do that," I said. Every time I came and helped Duffy in the garden, he made sure I took home some "leftovers" as he called them. One day it was lilies-of-the-valley; another time, it was tiny blue lobelia. The more I worked with Duffy, the more I began to understand flowers, their differences and the way flowers "talked." They could tell you if they were thirsty, or too dry, or feeling sick or overcrowded. He taught me how to take cuttings from his garden, and pretty soon the enchantment began to spill down from his garden into my tiny backyard. Everything I brought down from Duffy's flourished and bloomed. I waited for my mother to notice, but she never did.

"Oh, but I have to. Snapdragons get *snappish* if they're crowded. You have to humor snapdragons."

"You do?" I said, laughing. Duffy had such a funny way of saying things.

"Of course!" he answered, brandishing a pair of cutting shears and quickly snapping away until there were a dozen snapdragons on the ground at his feet. "Since snapdragons have mystical connotations, you have to be careful how you handle them."

"What do you mean, *mystical connotations*, Duffy? You mean like my T-shirt being enchanted, things like that?"

"Ah, you remembered. I thought perhaps you had refused to recognize the power, and it had slipped through your fingers. That will happen, you know. This whole garden was enchanted when Ruth and I first came here. I'm not sure it is anymore. . . ." he said, his voice trailing off. Then he continued, "But I thought everyone knew about snapdragons. For goodness sake, just look at the name: *dragons*, and *snapping* dragons at that! You can't get much more mystical, can you? How many dragons have you seen around here lately? They're not exactly running up and down the aisles of the supermarket, are they? No, no, snapdragons are *definitely* otherworldly."

"Duffy," I said—I had gotten used to calling him that, and it didn't seem disrespectful anymore—"how do you know about these things? I mean, you *are* just making this up, aren't you? Just for fun?"

"Am I making this up?" Duffy said, scratching his bristly chin like he was really trying to make up his mind about it. "No, I'm not making it up. You either know about these things or you don't. It's as simple as that."

I thought fleetingly of Mary's grandmother. "Do you know anybody else that knows about these things, Duffy?" I asked gently, trying not to hurt his feelings.

"Certainly! Not right in this neighborhood, maybe. Neighborhood's gone down as they say, that's for sure. Used to be everybody knew. . . ." He looked off into space for a moment as if he were seeing things that were invisible to people like me. Then he snapped back and looked at me very soberly with those piercing blue eyes. "Things change, Heather. Oh, I know that. Don't think I don't. Men weren't able to go to the moon when I was a boy. That's not true today. Does that mean it was a lie then? Of course not. Time was, when I was little, babies came from cabbages. That's what we were told. I still think it's a delightful idea. Never open a cabbagehead that I don't think about it. But that's all changed. We exchange things sometimes, fantasy for truth. Not necessarily a fair exchange. You ask your grandmother, she'd know."

I thought about my grandmother, and I wasn't sure she'd know at all. "My grandmother's different," I said. "She's not like you. . . . I mean, like most older people."

"And how are most older people?" he asked. "We're not all stamped out of a cookie cutter, you know. Old people are just like young people, Heather"—and then he paused for a moment before adding—"only they're wrinkled." We both laughed. "I must put these in water, or they'll wilt away right before our eyes," he said, gathering up the snapdragons and going into the kitchen.

I could see him through the window, and after a moment I followed him into the house.

"I think I know what you mean about old people being different from one another," I said. "It's just like young people are different, right?"

He nodded and continued slicing the stems of the snapdragons.

"I know some kids, they'll be nice little old ladies and gentlemen, I bet. But I know this girl Cathy Mercer, and I bet you anything she'll be an old stinker."

He laughed and continued fixing the flowers. I walked through to look at a curio cabinet in a corner of the dining room. I hadn't noticed it the first time I had been here, but then it was such a dark museum of a house, I suppose you could visit all the time and not notice things. In this cabinet there were little cups and saucers and china pitchers. Tiny, delicate dishes that looked like they belonged to a very elegant dollhouse. There was one thing I loved instantly: a miniature pitcher, pink with gold trim. It made me think of the tiny white flowers I had brought home from Mary's. They were lost in a juice glass that was much too big for them. They'd look so perfect in this tiny vase.

I hadn't heard him come up behind me until I saw his reflection in the glass.

"Like fairy things, aren't they?"

"They're beautiful. Just beautiful. But you have so many beautiful things!" I said, glancing over at the antique chairs and the pictures in their gilded frames. Unspoken was my next thought: Why don't you fix things up a bit? Open the windows, let some fresh air in! But it was as if he had read my thoughts. Or perhaps, as my mother always says, my face is transparent, showing everything I'm feeling.

"Ruth kept things so beautifully," he said. "I'm no good with this sort of thing," and he waved his hand to encompass just about everything in the house. "Lovely things outdoors I can deal with. But inside, I'm all thumbs. It seemed to me that every time I tried to clean things up a bit I broke something. And then I would think how sad Ruth would be. She loved every single object, the way I love my flowers. So one day I made a deal with the dust: I said, 'If you don't bother *me*, I won't bother *you*.' And you know what? We've gotten along just fine ever since. But sometimes I wonder what Ruth would say if she knew."

"How long, I mean, when did she. . . ?" I stumbled over the words. It was a simple question, but I felt that I was prying.

"Nine years ago. Nine years ago this autumn I've been alone. We had just moved into this house. I was finally going to take it easy and enjoy my retirement. But we were only here a few months when she took sick. Never forget the day the doctors told me there was no hope. I acted like a crazy man. That was the last day in October, and she was gone before Thanksgiving." He shook his head, as if to get rid of the bad memories. "See this," he said, opening the doors to the cabinet, "this little pitcher was one of Ruth's favorites," and he took out the pink and gold one I had been admiring.

I took it from him carefully, turning it around and examining the little fluted lip, the tiny curved handle. There were minute rosebuds circling the base. "It's the most exquisite thing I've ever seen," I said, handing it back to him.

He started to take it, and then his face lit up as if he had just had a wonderful idea. "No," he said firmly, "I don't want it."

"What?" I said, sure that I hadn't heard him right.

"No," he said, shaking his head to emphasize the point. "You must have it. A little girl like you will love it and show it off. That's what Ruth would want."

"Oh no," I said, "I couldn't." But even as I said it, I had to fight the impulse to clutch it tightly and run. My heart was thumping with excitement. "You really mean it?" I said.

"Of course I do. Let's just say it's my thank-you for all the work you've been doing. I'll have this place in fine shape for the garden tour, thanks to you."

"The garden tour?" I asked, following him back into the kitchen.

"Yes, yes," he said as he took the tiny vase from me and wrapped it in some paper towels. Then he got a paper bag and placed it inside, rolling it up tight. "Here, that should keep it till you get home," he said.

With the brown bag in one hand and the flowers in the other, I came back out into the sunlight. "I didn't know your house was on the garden tour," I repeated.

"Yes, yes," he said again, but his mind seemed to be far away. "You'd best hurry home now, before those dragons start snapping," and he ruffled my hair as he hurried me down the path.

When I got home, I put the snapdragons in a vase filled with water and set them in the middle of the dinette table. Then I unwrapped the china pitcher. Very carefully, I washed it and dried it with the kitchen towel. Now that it was cleaned up, it was even prettier. The white flowers were beginning to wilt, but they seemed to perk up as soon as I placed them in the tiny vase.

Looking at the flowers reminded me of Mary Tyson. I wanted to call her, but it was time to get things ready for supper.

I brought the flowers into my room and stood looking at my reflection in the mirror. I had forgotten I was wearing my Flower Power T-shirt. Maybe it was enchanted, after all.

Hadn't it brought me the most elegant thing I had ever owned?

If I had a grandfather, I decided, I would like him to be a lot like Duffy. I put the pitcher in a place of honor on my dresser, and I thought of all the things we'd talked about today. Men on the moon and snapping dragons. Deals made with dust and babies from cabbages. I loved the way Duffy talked. He had talked about something else today, something that had startled me. It was something important, I knew that, but it hid now in the back of my mind just out of reach, like a dream I couldn't remember.

I was setting the table for supper when Duffy's words came back to me. "Never forget the day the doctors told me there was no hope. I acted like a crazy man. That was the last day in October...." The last day in October. *Halloween!*

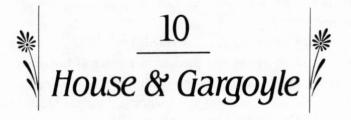

10

House & Gargoyle

They looked like withered old parsnips, dug up and chewed on by Tiger. But they weren't. They were called rhizomes, and they had beauty inside them. It was hard to believe, as I tucked each one into its proper place in my garden, that next summer there would be a row of irises where now there were just stubby green stalks. Another gift from Duffy! He had divided some of his beautiful purple irises and given me a dozen to line up along our fence. It was early in the morning, but I was anxious to get them in the ground.

As I finished and picked up my tools, I let out a sigh of satisfaction. The impatiens had been only the beginning. A cluster of them still stretched their rosy faces toward the sun, but they had been joined by forget-me-nots, daisies, lobelias, lilies-of-the-valley, and now irises. I was getting greedier as each week went by. I was what I'd always dreamed of being . . . a gardener!

I was so pleased with the sight in front of me that I let the phone ring twice before I dropped the water can and ran in to answer it.

"Hi, I'm back!"

"Lisa?"

"Were you asleep?"

"No, I was working in my garden."

"Very funny. Boy, do I have loads to tell you!"

"Yeah?"

"But I'll wait till we get together. What's new with you?"

I almost said, I've just told you what's new with me. I've got a garden! but I didn't. "Nothing much," I said.

"Want me to come over?"

"Of course! What time?"

"I can be there in half an hour."

"Great."

I hung up the phone, washed up, and dashed into my room. I threw the spread over my bed and smoothed it out with my hands. My mother said a long time ago that she didn't care how I made my bed as long as I made it. After all, I'm the one who has to sleep in it, right? So how I make it is very, very fast.

My shorts were muddy so I changed them, and then I combed my hair. I was sorry the Flower Power T-shirt was in the wash. I hadn't had a chance to show it to Lisa yet. The one I had on today was from last year, and it was getting a little small.

When I saw Lisa coming up the road, the first thing I noticed was how much lighter her hair had gotten. The second thing I noticed was how much darker her skin had gotten.

The third thing I noticed was the little paper bag in her hand.

"I brought you a souvenir," she said brightly.

"You didn't have to do that," I said. Why do I always say things I don't mean?

"Open it," she said.

It was a little seashell filled with dried flowers. They were tiny pink flowers, and they were tied with a pink ribbon.

"Oh, I love it!" I squealed. "Thank you so much!"

"You're welcome," she said, looking very pleased with herself. "I brought one home for Emily, too. She's not my best friend like you are, of course," she added hastily, "but since I couldn't go to her party, my mother thought I should bring her something."

We were sitting at the kitchen table, and I noticed she kept fluffing her hair while we talked.

"Your hair has gotten so blonde," I said.

"I *know*. It's sun-bleached," she said with a sigh.

"It looks terrific," I said truthfully. "And you're so tan."

"I *know*," she repeated. "I was swimming every day."

I could feel the old resentment rising in me. Why did Lisa make me feel like this? I thought of Mary . . . she didn't make me feel this way one bit. When she came to my house for lunch, she said she thought my room was pretty (which pleased me because I think so too, even if it's not very big), and when I showed her the little pink pitcher she said, "Oh, it's *darling!*"—in a way that made me feel she really meant it.

I pulled my attention back to Lisa. "So you had a good time, huh?"

"Oh, you better believe it. You know what I saw the other night? *The Beast and the Baby-sitter*. Was it gory!"

"That was one of the ones our folks wouldn't let us see," I said. "It's rated R."

"I know, but my cousin took me. She's only fifteen, but she looks older." Then, "Wouldn't let *who* see?"

"Mary and me. We saw *Champion Chimp* instead. It wasn't too bad. It was all about this professor who gives this magic stuff to a monkey, and the monkey becomes a genius and he becomes the president of the college and fires the professor. . . ."

"Mary Tyson?" she interrupted. "How come you went to the movies with her?"

"Well, she took the origami class with me, and then she was at Emily's, and then I had lunch at her house— Oh, I gotta tell you about the birthday party! We went to Liddonsville and went on all the rides, and wait'll I tell you what happened to Cathy Mercer. . . ."

"Let me tell you about *The Beast and the Baby-sitter* first," she said.

Before we had settled who got to talk first, the door opened, and Marshall walked in.

I had a whole bunch of reactions at once. First, I was glad that he had just walked in like he always had, which meant that maybe things hadn't changed too much after all; second, I thought he had his nerve just walking in like he always had, as if we were still friends; third, I wondered if he had come over because he knew Lisa was here (Lisa with the blonde hair and the tan); and fourth, I noticed how tanned and healthy *he* looked.

"Oh, I didn't know *you* were here," he said, spying Lisa. "See you later," he said to me, and he started to back out the door.

"Hey, wait a minute," I said, jumping up. "Don't run off. How're things?"

"Okay," he said, slumping against the doorjamb.

You didn't have to be brilliant to know that things weren't okay. Marshall looked awful. I know I said he looked tanned and healthy, and he did. Tanned and healthy and *awful*. He looked over at Lisa, and I could tell he didn't want to talk while she was there.

"So, what's new?" I said, stalling. "Go on any more camping trips?"

"Naw," he said, and again he looked over at Lisa, who was twisting one long blonde lock around her fingers. "I gotta go," he said finally, and that's what he did, turning and bolting across the yard connecting our two houses. I stood in the doorway and watched him disappear into his house. Then I came back in and sat down again with Lisa.

"What's the matter with him?" she asked.

"I dunno," I said.

"Marshmallow's always been weird."

"Yeah, well ..." I fingered the little shell with the pink flowers, and it reminded me that I wanted to show her the pitcher.

"Come into my room, I want to put this on my dresser and show you something."

She followed me, and I placed the shell on the dresser and picked up the pitcher.

"Isn't this beautiful?"

"Yeah," she said flatly. "Where'd you get it?"

"From Duffy," I said.

"Who?"

"Mr. Duffy. Remember, the old man who lives in the Reynolds' house? We met him in Brockmeyer's?"

"Oh yeah," she said, nodding.

"Lisa, he has the most beautiful garden you've ever seen."

"*My* mother would never let me go up there," she said.

"Well, to tell you the truth, Lisa, my mother wouldn't be too thrilled about it either, but she didn't really say I couldn't, so I just don't mention it. And Lisa, it's not true what they say about him. He's really very nice."

I told her everything then, starting with Tiger getting hurt and how scared I had been to go up there. I told her about Halloween, too: how his wife was dying and how upset he had been that night nine years ago. Now that it was all so clear, everybody would understand. I could tell she was impressed when I told her about the garden and the weeping willow and the pond. It made me feel good to be able to brag about something. I was even beginning to feel guilty that I had cut her off before she had a chance to tell me about *The Beast and the Baby-sitter*. I got so carried away that before I realized what I was saying, I blurted, "Would you like to go up there with me?"

"Gee, I don't know. . . ."

"Did your mother absolutely and positively tell you not to go up there?"

"No. I mean, we never talk about it. It's just always been so scary. Yeah, let's go!" she said, suddenly adventurous.

On the walk up to Duffy's, I let her tell me about her

grandfather's place and every single detail of *The Beast and the Baby-sitter.*

We circled the veranda and for a second, as we came into full view of the lawn, I couldn't see Duffy anywhere. But then I saw him. He was watering the clematis that climbed the fence bordering the pond, and he looked, as always, like a part of the landscape. I stopped Lisa at the top of the steps so she could be properly impressed.

"Well, what do you think? Isn't it gorgeous?" I realized that I was bragging about Duffy's garden the way Lisa usually brags about her grandfather's farm.

"It's nice," she said.

I looked over at her. Wasn't she impressed? Was I the only one who thought this place was special?

"Come on," I said. "I want you to meet him."

He saw me coming and stopped what he was doing while we made our way over to him.

"Hi," I said. He nodded, smiling, in that way he had of greeting me without saying a word. "Duffy, this is Lisa Pringle, my best friend."

"Hi," Lisa said.

Duffy didn't answer, but just stood there a moment looking at Lisa. Finally he said, "I guess you'll do."

"Pardon me?" she said.

"I said, 'You'll do.' For Heather's friend. Heather is a special person, and she can't have just anybody for a friend. But you knew that already, didn't you?"

Lisa nodded. "I . . . I guess so," she said, shooting me a glance that said, "We've stayed long enough. Let's get out of here."

"Duffy," I said, "Lisa's grandfather has a farm, and she's been up there for a whole month." I could feel Lisa preening at my elbow. "She knows a lot about gardens," I continued, "so I knew she'd appreciate yours. Is it all right if she looks around?"

"Of course. Gardens are to be enjoyed. Go ahead."

We started around the pond, and I could feel the garden embracing me the way it always did. The heavy scent of roses drifted over from the trellis, and I could hear the soft rustling sounds of chipmunks and squirrels darting about in the bushes.

"I think Duffy's garden looks like something you'd see in a book, don't you?"

"What kind of book?" Lisa asked.

"Well, you know, like in a fairy tale. It looks like . . . an enchanted garden," I heard myself say.

She shrugged her shoulders. "I guess so," she said grudgingly. "Except I don't like weeping willow trees. They're too droopy."

We had circled the pond and come back to where Duffy was working. He looked up at Lisa. She was wearing a T-shirt that said Springdale State Fair, and I saw him reading the words silently to himself. Oh no, here we go, I thought. . . . But he went back to his gardening without a word.

"Can I help?" I asked him.

"No, Heather, that's quite all right." Then, looking up at Lisa again, he said, "Heather's been helping me get ready for the garden tour." I suddenly felt uneasy.

"Oh? My mother works on that every year. This year

she's the chairperson," Lisa said. She was glancing around as she spoke, and following her glance, I noticed little things I hadn't seen before: a rusting sundial, places in the garden where the weeds were taking command, paint peeling off the picket fence. "Heather thinks your garden is enchanted," she said. "How did it get to be enchanted?" I wanted to kill her. Was she making fun of him?

But if Duffy knew he was being ridiculed, he didn't show it. "That's a secret," he said somberly. "Let's face it. If I knew, and I'm not saying whether I do or not, because I don't need a lot of news people and people from the television trampling all over the place, if I knew and I told, then everybody would be running around with enchanted gardens. And it wouldn't be so special anymore, would it? You wouldn't be at all impressed when Heather told you about it. Isn't that so? You'd say, 'So what? Isn't everybody's?' No, that's one of the most important rules I know: If you're lucky enough to have something you value, then it becomes enchanted, and you must guard it with your life. Never tell anyone the secret. And use the enchantment wisely. That's another rule. *Use the enchantment. . . .*"

Lisa hadn't moved while Duffy was talking, but now that he was silent, she nudged me. "We'd better get going," she said, "I've gotta get home."

"Oh yeah," I said.

We started for the stairs. "Thanks for letting me see your garden, Mr. Duffy," Lisa said politely.

"You're very welcome, Lisa. And it's Duffy. Just Duffy. Some of you young people have no manners," he said, smiling.

Lisa and I walked down to my house in silence, and when she left, neither of us had said anything about the afternoon. I wondered what she was thinking, but I was afraid to ask. Somehow I knew I'd find out soon enough.

An hour after she went home, the telephone rang.

"Heather? It's me."

"Hi, Lisa."

"Heather, my mother says she's going to talk to your mother. She says you shouldn't go up there anymore."

I could feel my face flush. I was going to find out what Lisa thought of Duffy, and it was going to be worse than I had imagined.

"Why not?" I asked angrily.

"Because he's crazy, Heather. All that talk about his garden being enchanted!"

"He is not crazy, Lisa! He just likes to talk that way."

"Well, even if he's not actually crazy, Heather, he's a big liar."

"What do you mean?"

"Remember he said his house was on the garden tour?"

"Yeah." I was getting a sinking feeling inside.

"Well, it *used* to be, sure, when the Reynolds lived there. But his garden's never been on the tour. He's let the place get so run-down"—there was a pause and I could hear her giggling—"that one of the ladies on the committee said now it's more like *House & Gargoyle.* Get it? Heather, are you listening?"

"I'm listening," I said. But I wasn't, really. I was thinking about Mary's grandmother.

"Heather, my mom says you must have been very lonely

or you wouldn't have bothered with someone like that. But don't worry, Heather, I'm home now. We'll do some great things together."

"Fine," I said.

"Maybe if I tell my mom you're not going up there again, she won't tell on you. Heather, should I tell her you promise?"

"What?"

"Promise not to go up there anymore, okay? Just promise."

"I promise."

11

Crazy Marshall

I was really mad at Lisa for spoiling things. Maybe that's not true: Maybe I was really mad at myself for bringing her up to see Duffy. I should have known she wouldn't understand. She didn't need Duffy the way I did, so she could see the weeds, and poke out the truth, and ruin everything. Because now I wouldn't go up there anymore. I just couldn't.

But Lisa was determined to keep me busy. We went bowling and to the movies, and one day we went shopping with Mrs. Pringle. But the best time I had that next week was one day when I went over to Mary's. We grilled hot dogs and sat around and talked, and then we took a swim in her neighbor's pool. When I got home, Lisa called.

"Where were you today?" she asked.

"I was over at Mary's."

"Where?"

"Mary Tyson's," I said. Why did Lisa make everything I did without her seem somehow . . . strange.

"Why'd you go *there?*"

I heard this really big sigh and realized it was coming from me. "Because she invited me. Why'd you think?"

"I didn't know you were going."

"She just called me this morning. It's not a big deal, Lisa."

"Well, I was trying to get you because I was going to have a picnic in my backyard. I had the paper plates and everything."

"Well, we can have it another day, can't we?"

"I don't know. The plates are left over from Bitsy's birthday party, and you know how she is. She probably won't let me use them another time."

It's funny when you get to know somebody. I could *hear* the expression on Lisa's face. Her voice got this pout in it, and I could tell exactly what she looked like.

"Well, I gotta go, Lisa," I said, and I hung up. I did have to start dinner, but really, I just didn't want her to ruin my good mood. It had been a fun day, and I didn't want her to spoil it like she spoiled everything else.

That night I did something I haven't done in a long time. I'm not sure why I did it, but when I was ready for bed, I asked Mom to come in and talk to me.

"Heather, what's happening to you?" she said, standing in the doorway.

"What do you mean?" I could feel my face getting red, as if I had done something stupid in front of the whole class.

"I *mean*, that ever since school's been out you've been acting strangely. The truth of the matter is, I think you've been regressing."

"I've been *what?*" It sounded like something you should be ashamed of.

"Regressing is, well, when someone goes backwards. When a girl is mature and self-reliant like you've always been, and she begins to act like a baby . . ."

"When did I act like a baby?"

"Oh"—this made my mother sit down on the bed at least—"not like a baby exactly, but, *dependent,* maybe that's the word I'm looking for. You've been asking me a lot of questions about where I'm going and when I'll be back and whether I have to work late again. I thought you always liked being on your own. Now all of a sudden you're a clinging vine. And you know how I feel about that!"

I felt as if I'd just had my face slapped. "Sorry" was all I could say, turning around in bed to face the wall.

"Oh come on, don't sulk. What did you want to talk about?"

"Nothing," I said. To myself I said, "There's a crazy old man up on the hill who pays more attention to me than you do."

"Well, okay. I have to do the payroll. Sleep tight. You're sure everything's okay?"

"Yeah," I said. But it wasn't okay. It took me a long time to get to sleep. I lay there feeling lonely and neglected and mad, all at the same time.

I hadn't spoken to Marshall since the day he came over when Lisa was here. I saw him a couple of times but either he was with Superdad or he and Ricky were doing something, and I didn't want to go over and say, "What was bothering you the other day?"

But one morning I saw him hosing out the garbage pails in his driveway. I waved and he didn't wave back, but I thought maybe that was because he hadn't seen me, so I went over.

"Hi, Marsh," I said, in my cheeriest voice. "Where you been? I hardly ever see you!"

"I've been around."

We were silent for a moment except for the *slosh slosh* of the water in the pails. I tried to stand far enough away that I wouldn't get sprayed by any of it.

"I guess you've been going all over the place with Su—with . . . uh, your stepfather, huh?"

"Naw," he said, and kept on sloshing.

Something was definitely wrong. For one thing, the old Marshall would have sprayed me with the hose by now. What was the matter with him?

"Is there something wrong, Marsh?"

"Naw. What could be wrong?"

What *was* wrong? I couldn't put my finger on it, but Marshall definitely was not himself. "Well . . . well, you're getting awfully stuck-up!" I said, and I turned and went back into my house.

I watched him for a while from the living room window, and it occurred to me that calling somebody stuck-up while they were hosing out a couple of garbage cans was not the brightest thing I had ever done.

While I watched, Mr. Teitelbaum came out of the house with his briefcase and hurried over to the car. Marshall dropped the hose and ran over to speak to him. I couldn't hear what they were saying, of course, but it looked as if Mr. Teitelbaum was real mad. He gestured to the hose, which was spilling down the driveway, and then drove away, leaving Marshall standing there looking desolate. He walked over and picked up the hose and resumed the washing of the garbage cans. Then suddenly he turned the hose around and started hosing down the windows, the porch door, the steps, everything in sight.

I stood there like a zombie, watching Marshall act like a crazy person. After a minute, he dropped the hose and went over and turned off the water. He sat down on the porch steps and just stared at his sneakers.

I couldn't stand it. I went out the back, and as slowly and quietly as I could, I walked over to where he was sitting. I don't know why I was being so cautious. I had never had to tiptoe around Marshall before. But then, he'd never acted so weird before. He'd never had a father before, either.

As I approached him, I saw what he was staring at. His sneakers were soaking wet. It would probably take a month for them to dry. He heard me and looked up suddenly. I thought for sure he'd be mad and yell something like "Get out of here!" but I guess hosing down the house had used up all his anger, and he just said "Hi."

"Hi, Marsh," I answered. Then I tentatively sat down next to him on the porch. I didn't realize until it was too late that the porch was soaking wet, and I had sat in a huge puddle. I could feel the cold water seeping right through my shorts, but I didn't want to jump up or say anything about the place being all wet, so I just sat there.

"How's things?" he said finally.

"Okay. How . . . how's things with you?"

He took a big sigh before he answered. "Lous-y!" he said.

"What's the matter?"

"Aw, nothing." I thought maybe he had decided not to tell me about it after all, but after a moment he said, "I hate him."

I swallowed hard. "Who?" I asked, which was dumb because of course I knew *who*, but I pretended I didn't.

"Him," he said.

The conversation was flowing like a piece of bubble gum stuck in your hair. "Your father?" I said finally.

"He's not my father," he said angrily, "he's my *step*father, and just because he married my mother doesn't give him the right to push me around. I wish he'd . . . he'd . . . go out of town on business—and *stay there*."

"But if he did, Marshall, you might have to go with him . . . away from here."

"No I wouldn't. I'd run away first. In fact, I might do that anyway."

"Oh come on, Marshall. It can't be that bad. I thought he was so great. He took you on that camping trip and everything." I hoped that the small joy I was feeling in Superdad turning out to be a dud didn't show in my voice. Because I didn't want Marshall to be unhappy, I really didn't.

"The camping trip was okay," he began, "but since then he's been awful. And my mom's changed, too. She agrees with everything he says." The words came spilling out of him now, as if he had been waiting to tell somebody how horrible it had been.

I began to get worried. Had he beaten Marshall? Was he really some kind of monster?

"Marshall," I said warily, squirming around in my wet shorts, "what's happened? What's he done?"

"Everything. And he won't let me do *anything*. You saw me. A hot summer day, and what am I doing? Cleaning out garbage cans. He only married Mom to get a slave. But she won't listen to me. He's the only one she cares about. I mean it, if it keeps up, I'm getting out."

"Marshall," I said, trying to pick my words carefully, "you're not going to run away because he made you clean out the garbage cans, are you?"

"It's not just the garbage cans. Don't you know anything, dummy? It's . . . it's . . . I *hate* him!"

He had jumped up and was kicking the hose around as he talked. "We were gonna do such great things together. Well, one camping trip is it. It's work, work, work. He's never home and when he is, all he does is yell at me."

I was glad he had gotten up because it gave me an excuse to get out of the puddle. "Gee, I'm sorry, Marsh," I said, trying the sympathetic approach. I had never seen him so upset. Except maybe the time Joey Herman stole his pet lizard. But then we were little, and he was able to cry. Now he wouldn't cry, and that made it harder. "You know who he sounds like?" I said, suddenly getting an idea.

"Who?" he said sullenly. "Darth Vader?"

"No, seriously, Joey Herman's dad. Remember how he used to yell and hit Joey? Luckily for Joey, his parents got divorced. Maybe the same thing will happen to yours!"

Marshall didn't say anything for a moment. "Naw, it's not

the same. I mean, he's never hit me," he said. "And I'd sure like them to get divorced, but I know my mom wouldn't like that."

"Marshall, maybe he just isn't used to being a father. You know, it happened to him pretty suddenly."

"Well, he's sure doing a lousy job of it. You could take anybody's father, and they'd be better at it than him."

"Not Joey Herman's," I said, teasing.

He grinned. It was a short one, but definitely a grin.

"No, not Joey Herman's." He picked up the hose as if he might start to roll it up, then dropped it again, as if he were too exhausted.

"You know what maybe you should do?" I said.

"What?"

"You know how people get trained for jobs? You know, like in those TV commercials, they call it on-the-job training. Maybe you could *train* him to be a good father!"

"What?" he said again.

"Sure. Figure out who's got a super father. You know, figure out which one of your friends has a father you could train him to be like."

"That's a dumb idea, Heather. Really dumb."

"No it isn't, Marsh. It's better than running away."

"Maybe."

I wanted to go home and change, so I said, "I'll see you later, okay?"

"Right," he said, and I turned and started toward my house. But I had only gone a few steps when an icy stream of water hit my back like a bullet.

"Marshall!" I gasped, turning to scream at him. But that

was a mistake, because then I got it down my front. Sputtering and squealing, I retreated to my own backyard. Shivering, I yelled over, "I'll get you for that, Marshall Teitelbaum."

But he only laughed and started rolling up the hose. And I laughed, too, because I knew Marshall was Marshall again.

12

The Training of Teitelbaum

"I'll try not to be late tonight," Mom said as she searched for her car keys. "It's just these darn summer sales."

"That's okay, Mom."

"Are you sure you don't want to walk in and have lunch with me in town?"

"No, really, Mom. Thanks anyway."

It had been like this ever since that night in my room. I've been trying not to ask Mom any more questions, or act the least bit babyish, even though I wasn't aware I was doing it. I feel guilty because obviously I've made *her* feel guilty. Now she's questioning our whole lifestyle because I wanted her to tuck me in bed. Once . . . just once.

The morning that she asked me if I wanted to meet her for lunch was the morning Marshall showed up at the kitchen door five minutes after she had left.

"Hi," he said.

"Hi."

We stood awkwardly for a moment, and then I moved

back and he came in and went right to the refrigerator.

"It's almost as empty as ours," he said.

"What's the matter, don't they feed you over there?" I said, laughing. But as soon as I said it, I knew Marshall didn't think it was very funny.

He glared at me. "Just you shut up, okay?"

"Marshall, what's the matter with you? I was only kidding!"

He stared at the floor for a moment. "Aw, I'm sorry," he said.

I couldn't have been more surprised. Almost anything Marshall could have said wouldn't have surprised me as much as his saying that simple "I'm sorry." Marshall never apologized. He used to say that all the time, whenever he got in trouble: "I *never* apologize." It was his code of honor.

I sat down and didn't say anything. Obviously, Marshall was becoming a whole new person, and I wasn't sure how I felt about that. First the tirade last week, now apologizing to me. When he took out some bologna and cheese, I said, "The bread's in the top drawer."

He let out an exasperated sigh. "I know where the bread is," he said.

He hadn't been around much this summer, so I wasn't sure he did, but I said, "Of course you do, Marshall."

When he sat down, I gave him time to finish half the sandwich, and then I couldn't stand it anymore.

"Is everything horrible?" I asked.

He shook his head. "Naw," he said, taking another huge bite out of his sandwich.

"Well, is it any better than it was before?"

"Naw," he said again, stuffing the last of the sandwich into his mouth.

"Marshall, talk to me. What's happening? Why are you so hungry?"

"He eats *health food*," he said, wiping his mouth with his wrist. "And he's getting Mom the same way. You could search my house for a week, and you wouldn't find anything that tastes good. I've forgotten what a Twinkie looks like."

"Gee, that's awful," I said.

"I thought about what you said, about, you know, training him to be a good father?"

"Yeah?"

"And I don't think it'll work."

"Why not?"

"He's too dumb."

The phone rang, and I jumped to answer it.

"Hello?"

"Hi, Heather. What're you doing?" It was Lisa.

"Marshall's here. We're just talking."

"Oh. Then I guess it's not such a good idea."

"What's not such a good idea?"

"My coming over."

"I didn't know you were coming over."

"My dad is doing some errands this morning, and he could drop me off for a while. But if Marshall's there . . ."

With the mention of Lisa's dad, a light bulb went off in my head, just like you see in the cartoons.

"No, I think it's a great idea," I said. "Come on over." I hung up the receiver. "Lisa's coming over," I said brightly.

"Good-bye," Marshall said, rising from the chair.

"Don't go! You're the reason I told her to come."

"Me?"

"How can you train Teitelbaum to be a good father if you don't know anything about a good father? Remember when I had the idea, I said you had to model him after somebody? Well, Lisa's father is as good as anybody's."

"It won't work," he said, looking in the cupboards as we talked. This time he took out the peanut butter and jelly and went to work.

"Marshall, it's worth a try. What do you have to lose? Here, what we have to do," I said, fishing in the catchall drawer for a piece of paper and a pencil, "is make a list of questions to ask Lisa. Questions about her father. That'll be our guide." I found an old envelope and the stub of a pencil. Marshall had settled himself down with the peanut butter and jelly sandwich and a glass of grapefruit juice. "That's a disgusting combination," I said.

"You're out of milk."

"What'll we do for the first question?" I asked.

"This is a stupid idea," he said.

"Marshall, don't be so stubborn. What are the things about him that bother you the most?"

He stretched himself out in the chair so that his legs were tipping over the chair on the other side.

"Don't knock over the chair, Marsh," I said.

"Why not?"

"*Because*. Answer my question." It occurred to me that I sounded like Mrs. Burns, the library aide.

"He does everything wrong," he said finally.

"But you've got to be specific if this is going to work."

"Well, he eats all that junk."

Next to the big (*1*) on the page I wrote, *Does not provide proper food for son.*

"Wait a minute," I said. "That's a complaint, not a question. Maybe we should do it that way. Just list the complaints. What else?"

Marshall had his glasses down on the tip of his nose, and he was wiggling them up and down like he always does when he's bored. "He's always criticizing me," he said, "and he yells a lot."

"Wait a minute," I said, "that's two things." I wrote (*2*) *Always crit*—"How do you spell *crit* . . . never mind." I wrote, *Picks on son.* And for (*3*), *Yells a lot.* "Go on," I said, feeling like we were finally making progress.

"Works me like a dog. Like a *slave*," he corrected.

"(*4*) Makes son work too hard. What else?"

"I dunno. . . ."

"How about your mother? Does he treat her okay?"

"Yeah. They get along fine. That's what makes it so bad."

I looked at him. "What do you mean?"

"Well, she sides with him all the time. I don't think she even likes me anymore." He paused for a moment. "I think she might even hate me by now, the way it's been going."

"Gee, Marsh. I'm sorry."

I heard something behind me and turned to see Lisa framed in the kitchen window. I waved her in.

"Hi, you guys. Whatcha doing?"

Marshall made a face, so I tried to be tactful. "We're just talking, Lisa, that's all."

She sat down on one of the other kitchen chairs, and for a

moment the three of us just sat there in silence. Then Marshall jumped up. "I gotta go," he said.

I grabbed his arm. "No you don't, Marshall. Come on. We can just talk a little," I said. He shrugged his shoulders and stood leaning against the counter. "Lisa," I said, "Marshall and I were just talking about fathers."

"Huh?" she said.

"We were talking about fathers. I mean, now he has one, just like you." I put on my brightest tone of voice, but I knew it was a dopey way to begin.

"Oh yeah. How's it going? It must be neat, huh?" she said, with this real goopy look on her face.

I got nervous for a moment. Don't explode, Marsh, I begged him silently. Be nice.

By way of an answer, Marshall grunted.

"Lisa," I said, "what's your father like?"

"You know what my dad's like."

"Well, we're kind of comparing fathers, you know? To see how Mr. Teitelbaum compares to other fathers. Like . . . like what kind of food does yours like?"

"Food? *Weird* stuff," she answered.

"What do you mean?"

"Like little wrinkled green things he puts in his salad. He's always talking about cholesterol and how he has to keep his weight down. I think he'd let me starve to death before he'd order a pizza. He never used to be this way. I think he's getting old."

I looked at Marshall, but his face was a blank. I glanced down at the crumpled envelope in my hand and fired off my next question. "I guess it must be nice to have a father around to pay you compliments," I said. I thought I was being devilishly clever.

"I wouldn't know," she said wearily. "This morning, so far, he's told me my hair is too messy, my shorts are too short, and he pointed out where I had dribbled milk . . . on my *white* T-shirt. And he was in a good mood today."

Somehow this wasn't going the way I had planned. "But he doesn't *yell*, does he?"

"Only when he wants me to get off the phone. Or when he wants me to turn down the radio. Or when . . . hey, what are you doing, taking a survey? You're getting me awfully depressed."

"Does he make you work? I mean, do you have to wash out the garbage cans?" I asked desperately. My idea wasn't so good, after all!

Lisa made a face. "Of course not," she said. "What kind of monster do you think he is?" I settled back in my chair. Now we were getting somewhere. "He makes my *brother* do that," she said.

I glanced up at Marshall, but he was still slouched against the counter looking bored.

"My mom's the one who makes me work," Lisa continued. "Make your bed, set the table, walk the dog." It was as if I had tapped a wellspring in Lisa and all the complaints were coming out. I felt guilty. Lisa had walked in here perfectly happy with her parents, and now she was going to be as miserable as Marshall. And I hadn't done Marshall any good, either. Lisa's father was just as bad as his.

"Lisa," I said, "I thought your father was terrific."

"Well, I guess he is. But he's still a *father*, Heather. Marshall knows what I mean. Don't you, Marshall?"

"Marshall?" I said, looking up at him.

He pushed his glasses back up on his nose and cleared his throat. "Yeah?" he said.

"What d'you think?"

"I told you it was a stupid idea," he said. "I gotta go," he said then and went out, slamming the door behind him.

"What was all that about?" Lisa asked.

"Oh, Marshall's having a little trouble with Mr. Teitelbaum," I said.

"Why? Because he yells and picks on him? All fathers do that."

I looked at Lisa blankly for a moment. "They do?" I said.

"Of course they do, Heather."

"Well, I guess Marshall just doesn't know that," I said. But maybe he does now, I thought. Maybe he does now. . . .

13

Empty Gardens

I sat in the back seat of the Pringles' car feeling stiff and overdressed. I know it was silly to feel overdressed when all I was wearing was a sundress, but I live in shorts all summer. But Lisa's mother said we *had* to wear dresses if we were going to help on the tour.

Lisa was very excited about it, because ordinarily only teenagers are allowed to help. She said they were making a special exception for her because Mrs. Pringle is the chairperson. And the special exception was extended to include me, I guess because I'm the chairperson's daughter's best friend.

When Lisa first told me about it, I wasn't sure how I felt. The garden tour reminded me of Duffy, and I tried not to think about him. It had been almost three weeks since I'd seen him, and I wondered if he missed my visits. I tried to tell myself that he probably didn't; I also told myself that he wasn't up there today waiting for people to come and admire his garden. If I thought he was, I'd feel so sad I couldn't stand it.

We were assigned to work at the Anderson home, a big brick house on the outskirts of Oakfield. Mrs. Pringle had coached us in what we were to do: When people arrived at the house, we were to check that they were wearing a little yellow badge in the shape of a rose. That meant they had paid at one of the other houses. If they didn't have a badge, that meant that the Andersons' was the first house they were visiting, and we were to direct them to the table inside where two ladies were collecting admission.

We stood for about two hours at the top of the Andersons' driveway. Everybody had to leave their cars down at the bottom of the hill and they were out of breath by the time they climbed to the top. Almost everybody we saw had the little rose badge, so it was pretty boring. I wanted to look around at the gardens, but Lisa said we couldn't budge from our post.

"Aren't you tired of standing in one spot?"

"No," Lisa said primly.

"Well, I am," I said. There was a statue of a man with no clothes on holding a big bowl of water. I think it was intended to be a birdbath but since there wasn't any water in it, I went over and sat on the rim.

"Heather, you're not supposed to do that!"

"Why not?"

"Because it's a birdbath."

"Well, if any birds come along, I'll move."

"But it doesn't look . . . dignified."

"Who wants to look dignified?"

Lisa and I don't seem to see things, or *feel* things, the same way anymore. I thought about Marshall and what he would do with a birdbath. Probably swim in it. I used to think things were different with Lisa because I wasn't used to having a girl for a best friend. Lately I'm not so sure.

A fat lady was coming up the hill, and her face was getting redder and redder by the minute. She was huffing and puffing like a steam locomotive by the time she got up to where we were waiting. I hopped off the birdbath and smoothed down my skirt.

The woman was the fattest person I had ever seen. Her dress hung down almost to her ankles, so that she didn't seem to have any legs as she approached us. She was wearing a big straw hat with yellow daisies on it.

"Good afternoon," Lisa said in a singsong voice. I was looking for the little yellow badge. Usually it was easy to spot, but this lady was so huge, it was like hunting for a polka dot on a parachute.

"Excuse me, if you haven't already paid, the admission desk is around at the back door," I said.

The woman was huffing and puffing so much she could barely speak. "We've paid," she said, gesturing to the woman beside her. Her companion was older than she was, but half her size, and she remained silent. Neither of them had a rose badge.

Lisa glanced over at me nervously.

I cleared my throat. "May we see your rose badge?" I asked.

"We're wearing them," the fat lady said mischievously.

My eyes darted over her voluminous form once again. "You *are?*"

"Certainly," she said, and her hand popped up to the straw hat on her head. She plucked two plastic yellow roses from among the daisies and said "See?" with a big guffaw.

I smiled with relief. I hadn't wanted to throw my body across the driveway to bar her admittance if she tried to sneak in. Of all the people who couldn't sneak in, I thought.

"Go right in," I said. As I watched her waddle around the corner, I suddenly thought of Duffy and what his reaction would be. I could just hear him saying, "Is your straw hat enchanted?"

"I've gotta go to the bathroom," I said to Lisa.

She shook her head. "You're not allowed to, I don't think."

"What do you mean, I'm not allowed to?"

"Only the guests are allowed to use the rest rooms."

"Lisa, I'll wet my pants if I don't go. How would your stuffy old committee like that?"

"The committee is not stuffy. My mother's on the committee, and you're being *crude.*"

"I am not!" I said, starting for the back door. I knew the kitchen was in there, so the bathroom couldn't be far away. "If I went in the birdbath," I called over my shoulder, "*that* would be crude!"

When I came into the kitchen, the first thing I noticed was that I couldn't see very well because I'd been out in the sun, so I stood for a moment letting my eyes get accustomed to the inside. It was nice and cool in the kitchen, just like Duffy's house. You didn't get that cool feeling in my house, or Lisa's. It must be something about a big old house.

"Can I help you?" someone asked me in a harsh, strong accent.

I looked up to see a lady with a flower pinned to her dress peering down at me through thick glasses. She had the glasses tied to a string so she wouldn't lose them.

"I . . . I was just looking for the girls' room," I said.

She smiled, but her teeth were crooked and brown, so she didn't smile for very long. If I had teeth like that, I'd never smile. *Never.*

"Right through there," she said, pointing around the corner.

After I came out of the bathroom, I stood for a moment looking around. The kitchen, and the entrance out to the driveway where Lisa was waiting, was to my right. I turned to my left.

I came into the biggest hallway I had ever seen (except in a movie). It was painted dark red, and there was an old painting on the wall of somebody from about two hundred years ago. There was a big marble staircase, and I would have died to go upstairs and see what was up there. Luckily there was a rope placed across it to keep out trespassers. Even *I* wouldn't jump over a rope or crawl under it. Then you'd really be in trouble. If somebody caught me now, I could just say I was lost. There were people coming down the hall. I walked as tall as I could and sailed right by them. After all, I was working here, wasn't I? I had a right to look around. What was the good of having a tour, if you didn't get to tour?

There was a dining room with a long, carved table all set for dinner. I counted the places. There were fourteen places set. And there were extra chairs lined up along the walls. This must be a mansion. I didn't even know there were houses like this in Oakfield. The living room was the same kind of room, with everything very elegant. There was a piano in one corner of the room—that was how big the room was: A piano fit into the corner very neatly tucked away, so you didn't have to notice it if you didn't want to. Most rooms, a piano would hog the whole room. There were more portraits on the wall; I guess the Andersons have a very distinguished family tree. We have some pictures of my ancestors, but none of them are dressed like these people. Maybe the pictures we have aren't old enough, but I have a hunch even if they were, my ancestors didn't dress like these people. Or have their portraits painted. The oldest picture we have is one of my great-great-grandmother, and she's just sitting in a chair by a fireplace peeling potatoes. I don't think any of the Anderson ladies ever peeled potatoes.

After I had looked around a little more, I made my way back outside.

"Where've you been?" Lisa asked. I was pleased to see that she was leaning on the birdbath.

"I was looking around. You should see the inside. It's a real mansion!"

"I know. I've been here before," she said.

"Oh."

"My mother went to a luncheon here once."

"Oh."

"My mother's going to a luncheon over at Fairview next week. It's going to be *really* fancy."

"Oh . . ."

At four o'clock the tour was over, but before we left, Mr. and Mrs. Anderson came out to thank Mrs. Pringle and Lisa and me. The Andersons were about two hundred years old. The portraits on the walls could have been of *them*.

I walked around and looked at the garden before I left. It was very stiff and formal and quiet, just like the house. The flowers were so proper and well behaved, they didn't even bump into one another. Lined up in rows, hundreds of irises, gladiolus, and larkspur marched along the paths one behind the other, with their heads held high like stuck-up schoolgirls. I didn't hear a bird chirping or a bee buzzing. It seemed empty to me, but maybe it was just meant to be dignified. I don't think a garden should be either of those things: empty *or* dignified.

When I got home, I went out in back and sat in *my* garden. It certainly didn't look too impressive after this afternoon, but I loved it. There were enough flowers now for me to cut bouquets. I had little bunches of marigolds and zinnias scattered throughout the house.

I wondered what Duffy was doing. Was there something wrong with me, to think his garden was nicer than the Andersons'? True, his house was dusty and cluttered and a little strange; there were weeds in his garden; and according to Lisa, Duffy talked crazy. But so what? It occurred to me that I had never found out what Duffy thought about Lisa.

I remembered how Duffy had described his mind as being like a house with too much furniture in it. That's the way my head felt now: crowded and confused. I looked around for Tiger. Where was he? I hadn't seen him in the house. Of course, he was probably sleeping under my desk, as usual. But maybe he wasn't. Maybe he had wandered off again. And if he had, shouldn't I go look for him?

I would only stay for a minute. Maybe if I was lucky, I would see the house the way everybody else seemed to see it, and I'd know that Mrs. Pringle and the committee were right. And I wouldn't miss Duffy anymore.

I hurried down the road, the sun shimmering through the trees ahead of me. I'd have to make it a quick visit; Mom would be home soon.

As I went up the steps, I rehearsed what I would say.

"Is Tiger here? I thought he might have wandered up."

If he asks where I've been, should I just explain that I've been very busy? With what? But somehow, even as I worried about it, I knew Duffy wouldn't ask me. He would never try to make me feel guilty.

I rounded the veranda and the first thing I noticed was the stillness. I stopped at the top of the steps and searched the garden for the familiar figure in the battered hat, but the garden was empty. I heard a "meow," and felt Jezebel rubbing against my leg. Scooping her up, I stood petting her, still not moving. I looked down at the garden again, hoping that he would materialize if I gave him a second chance. But he wasn't there.

He was inside the house then, maybe resting or fixing his dinner. Could he be out somewhere? Why did it seem so wrong for Duffy not to be in his garden? He was *supposed* to be there; I needed him to be. But I hadn't been here in a while. I had no right to expect anything.

Gently I put Jezebel down and turned to go, but she went over to the kitchen door and began to scratch. There was something about her mewing that made me stop. I walked over to the door, but I felt foolish, as if I would be intruding on Duffy.

Finally, I decided to knock. As I did, I peered through the glass for the first time, and my hand froze.

Duffy was lying face down on the kitchen floor. He was lying very still, like a dead person.

14
Don't Panic!

I don't know how long I stood there, my hand leaning against the glass. I felt a buzzing in my ears, and I had this strange feeling that the scene in front of me was unreal, a *nightmare*, and I was going to wake up. Then, without realizing I was doing it, I turned the knob and went in.

Jezebel brushed past me, mewing pitifully, and made a beeline to where Duffy was lying. I just stood still for a moment. Part of me wanted to turn and run, and not stop running until I was far away from here. I felt a tightness in my throat, and my heart was pounding so hard I thought it would burst through my chest. Slowly, I inched over to the figure on the floor and peered down into his face. Was he alive? He was lying over on his side, his glasses half on and half off. Strangely, I wasn't as frightened when I saw him close up. It was Duffy, and he looked as if he were sleeping. He was very still, but he *had* to be alive. I willed him to be.

I knew I had to stay calm. That's what Mom always told me to do in an emergency. "Don't panic!" she used to say,

"Panic scrambles your thinking. Just *stay calm and do what has to be done.*" Suddenly I was able to move.

I went to the phone on the wall, dialed 0, and listened impatiently as it rang one, two, three times.

"Operator."

"Operator, I need an ambulance."

"What is the matter?"

"There's an old man, and he's on the floor. I think maybe he's had a heart attack. Please, send someone right away!"

"What is the address?"

"The old Reynolds' place at the end of Lehigh Street. They'll know it."

"Please stay on the line."

I heard her click off, and there was silence for what seemed like an eternity. Finally she came back on.

"An ambulance is on its way. Who is this calling, please?"

"My name is Heather Mallory," I said slowly, and as my name echoed in the silent room, I could hear Duffy's voice, the way he used to say my name, and suddenly the tears came. I hung up the phone and turned my face to the wall. I knew he couldn't hear me or see me; I knew that no one could. Still I wanted to hide. I had never felt so awful in my life, so ashamed.

After I had cried for a minute, I felt a little better. I dried my face with the back of my hand and looked over at Duffy. I wanted to put something under his head to make him comfortable, but I knew that I shouldn't try to move him. I went and looked at him carefully again. What if he were already dead? What if all this time, I was calling an ambulance for doctors to come and care for a dead man?

His hand lay open on the floor, and I remembered what I had learned about taking a pulse. Gingerly I reached over and placed my finger where the pulse should be. I felt nothing. An icy fear crept over me. I moved my finger slightly. Again nothing. And again I moved my finger and pressed just a little. Then I felt it. It was faint, as if it were very far away, but Duffy had a pulse. Duffy was alive.

I stood up and just as I did, I heard the loud wail of the ambulance coming down the road. I ran out the door to meet the ambulance driver and show them where to come.

When I got to the driveway, a short stocky man got down from the driver's seat.

"You the person who called?" he said brusquely.

I nodded.

"Show us," he said.

I hurried back up the steps with the men pounding up behind me. I held the door open as they filed in with the stretcher. As the first man knelt beside Duffy, I blurted, "He's still alive. I felt his pulse."

They seemed to be ignoring me now, barking orders to one another as if I weren't even there. They placed Duffy on the stretcher with an oxygen mask strapped to his face and started out the door.

"Are you his granddaughter?" the driver asked me, more gently now.

I shook my head. I could feel a huge lump coming into my throat, and I didn't trust myself to speak.

"Does he live alone?" he asked.

I nodded. "I . . . I'm just a neigh— a friend of Mr. Duffy's," I said.

"Do you know if he has any relatives?"

"I don't think so."

We had gone down the steps and the driver jumped into the front seat.

"Can I come with you?" I asked. I hadn't known I wanted to go, but the thought of Duffy being taken to the hospital by strangers was unbearable.

"No, I'm afraid not, miss." But he smiled at me. "You've done very well."

Then he slammed the door and with the siren piercing the air once more, they headed down the driveway and were out of sight.

I turned back and went inside the house. Everything looked perfectly normal. There was a coffee cup in the sink, and I washed and dried it and put it in the cupboard. Then I walked into what Duffy called the parlor, where the shades were drawn as always against the afternoon sunlight. It was after five o'clock now, and the room was shadowed and sad. There was a newspaper lying on the chair, and I folded it before putting it in the magazine rack.

Suddenly I shivered. What right did I have to be here? I wasn't Duffy's friend. Friends don't desert each other. I ran out, locking the kitchen door with the key Duffy kept in the flowerpot, and hurried down the hill.

It felt good to get home. It was almost five thirty, but I remembered that Mom was working until seven tonight so I didn't have to rush dinner. In fact, when I checked the refrigerator, I realized we had enough left over from last night, and I didn't have to cook at all. Which didn't help matters. I needed something to keep me busy. The telephone rang.

"Guess what? I got a new bathing suit!"

"Lisa?"

"It's gorgeous! Remember I told you I saw one that I loved, but it was too expensive? Well, we stopped at Dalton's on the way home, and it was on sale, and . . ."

I couldn't let her go on. "Lisa, shut up. Duffy's hurt."

"*What?*"

I could tell by her voice that Lisa wasn't shocked as much as she was annoyed. Annoyed that I had interrupted her.

"I went up to see him and he was lying on the floor, unconscious. I called the ambulance, and they took him to the hospital."

"Oh gosh, how *creepy*. Weren't you scared?"

"Well, a little, at first."

"Why'd you go up there? I thought you weren't going to be friends with him anymore."

I could feel my throat getting tight. Lisa was making me mad, and she was making me feel guilty all over again. Lisa never felt the way I did about things. How could I have let her change the way I feel about somebody? How hurt had Duffy been that I hadn't come to see him?

"Good-bye, Lisa," I said simply and hung up the phone.

I stood there for a moment, hanging on to the handle of the wall phone as if it were holding me up. Then I lifted the receiver and dialed Marshall's number.

"Hello."

"Marsh, it's me."

"Hi. What's up?"

"Marsh, can you come over?"

There was a pause, and I almost hung up. If there was no one I could talk to, no one who had the same kind of feelings that I had, I would die. Then I heard him say "Sure," and he hung up.

I walked over to the window and almost immediately Marshall's back door opened, and he came bounding out. I don't remember ever being so glad to see someone. He burst in the door before I had a chance to open it.

"What's wrong?" he said, panting for breath.

I bit my lip. I felt like crying again, and I didn't want to in front of Marsh. "Nothing," I said.

He collapsed in the kitchen chair. "What d'ya mean, nothing? I busted my can getting over here. You sounded like you were in some kind of trouble."

I walked over and pulled out the chair opposite him.

"I . . . I just needed to talk to someone." He didn't say anything. I think he was still trying to catch his breath. "Remember Duffy, Marsh? The old man who lives in the Reynolds' house?"

"Yeah?"

"Well." I swallowed hard but it wasn't any use. The tears came with the words, and I sniffled and choked and made dreadful sounds while I tried to tell him what had happened. He just listened.

"I know he wasn't any relative or anything, and you must think I'm so stupid, but Marshall, I liked him and he liked me and made me feel good, and you were away and Lisa was away, and even when she's here, and she said I shouldn't go up there and I didn't and then when I did, oh Marshall, what'll I do if he dies? It's all my fault!"

Marshall let out a loud sigh. "You're such a dummy. I can't understand half of what you're saying. Now take it easy and talk slow." He reached over and grabbed a napkin from the napkin holder. "Here. Your nose is running all over your face."

I blew my nose and calmed down a little. Then I told him the whole story, not sparing myself a bit because I felt like the rottenest person in the whole world. When I was finished, he said, "I don't know why you feel so bad. You probably saved his life."

I sniffed and looked at him. He was only trying to make me feel better, of course, but I had never thought about that.

"If you hadn't gone up there, bingo! Who else would have? They probably wouldn't have discovered the body for weeks. I read in the paper about this guy. . . ."

I shook my head. "Don't Marsh. I don't want to hear one of your grisly stories. Do you really think I saved his life?"

He nodded. "Sure."

"But what if he dies?"

"Then you *didn't* save his life," he answered.

In spite of myself, I giggled.

"I have to find out how he is. I don't even know what's wrong with him."

"Why don't we call the hospital?"

"Marshall, that's a great idea!"

"Of course," he said. "*I* thought of it."

I got the telephone book and looked up the number of Valley Hospital. As I picked up the receiver, I looked questioningly over at Marsh. "What'll I say?"

He made a face. "Heather, don't be so dumb. If you were able to call an ambulance and everything, you'll know what to say."

Marshall was right. I had to stop acting like a little kid. I was almost twelve. I dialed the number, and when the voice said "Valley Hospital," I said, "I have a friend who was just taken to the hospital in an ambulance. I would like to check on his condition."

"One moment, please." There was a click, and a pause and then, "Desk."

"I have a friend who was just taken to the hospital in an ambulance. I would like to know how he is, please."

"What is the name?"

"Thomas Duffy."

"Are you a relative?"

"No, just a friend."

"One moment, please."

I heard a click, and my hand tightened on the receiver. *What if they tell me he's dead . . . ?* I felt so nervous I was ready to explode.

The voice came back on the line. "The patient is in the intensive care unit."

"Is . . . is he going to be all right? What's wrong with him?"

"We can't give out any further information at this time, but his condition is listed as stable."

"Thank you," I said, and hung up. I repeated the conversation to Marshall.

"That's good," he said.

"It is?"

"Sure. *Stable* means, you know, he's doing okay."

I could feel my body relax. "You think so?"

"Of course. Everybody knows that. Ask your mom." He nodded toward the door, and I turned as my mother came in.

"Gosh, is it seven o'clock already?" I asked.

"No, hon, I quit early. Hi, Marsh. What's up?"

I took a deep breath. I wasn't sure I was ready to go over it all again with my mother now that I had finally calmed down.

Marshall got up and made for the door. He paused in the doorway and gave my arm a punch. "See ya tomorrow."

"Thanks, Marsh," I said.

When I turned around my mother was studying me silently.

"Heather, have you been crying? What's happened?" she asked, sounding frightened.

"Oh, *Mom*," I said, feeling the tears spilling over again. Would I never stop crying?

But it felt almost *good* to cry this way, with my mother holding me tight, stroking my hair and saying "It's okay, it's okay" the way she did when I was a little girl.

15
Using the Enchantment

Duffy had suffered a stroke. That's what the doctor told Mom. (They wouldn't tell *me* anything.)

We had learned in health last year that when a person has a stroke, the blood supply is interrupted somewhere along the way and doesn't reach a part of their brain. A person can be hurt real bad by a stroke: Some people are paralyzed; some have trouble speaking. It depends on what part of the brain is damaged. But lots of people get better with therapy, and Duffy was going to be one of those people.

Dr. Barker said that Duffy must have collapsed just before I got there, and my finding him right away really helped his chances a lot. He would have problems. He would have a limp, and he might have some trouble with his arm. But Duffy was alive, that was the most important thing. Duffy was alive!

One night after it happened, Mom came in and sat down on the edge of my bed just before I switched out the light.

She hadn't said anything when I told her I had been going up to Duffy's, and I wondered if that's what she wanted to talk to me about now.

"Heather," she began, and then she seemed to hesitate, as if she didn't know how to continue. "I'm sorry," she said.

I waited for her to go on, but she just sat there, winding a strand of blanket fuzz around her finger.

"What are you sorry about?" I said. *Sorry you've got such a sneaky daughter?*

"I may have ... cheated you. And I never intended that." I didn't say anything. "Heather, I didn't want you to grow up helpless, dependent, coddled ... call it what you like. I was brought up like that. And when your father was killed"—here she took a deep breath—"I was *devastated*. Can you understand what I'm saying? It was as if I had built a fine big house to live in—everything perfect, everything exactly as I had planned, and then in one night it was gone, burned to the ground. That's what I felt had happened to my life. And you know what somebody has to do when that happens?" I shook my head. "*Rebuild*. And that's what I did. I rebuilt my 'house,' but not the same as before. This time the only thing that mattered to me was that it was fireproof. No frills, no dreams. I didn't want to be hurt again, and I didn't want you to be hurt. I tried to make you self-reliant, able to take care of yourself. But maybe I overdid it. When I think how you were drawn to that old man, simply because he paid attention to you!"

"But you pay attention to me!" I protested.

"But maybe not enough, or not in the right way." She

touched her fingers to my face. "It's fine to be responsible. But I never let you just be a *child.*"

She reached out then, and we sat there hugging each other in silence. Then I thought of something that might make her feel better.

"Mom, when I first saw Duffy, I wanted to run away. I was scared, you know? But then I remembered what you told me about handling an emergency, and I felt better."

"You did, really?"

"Really. So you see, you're not a hopeless failure after all."

She pushed me down in bed, and we laughed.

"You have no respect for your elders. Go to sleep. I just wanted to get that off my chest."

"Anytime," I said.

She shook her head at me, but I think she felt better. I know I did.

A few days later, Mom came into the kitchen while I was eating breakfast. She eyed me critically for a moment and then she asked, "Okay, baby, I can't stand it anymore. Why are you wearing it?"

I looked up at her, widening my eyes to show I didn't know what she was talking about. "What do you mean?"

"Why are you wearing that T-shirt Grandma sent you *for the fifth day in a row?* I know you like it, but five days is a bit much, even for you."

I swallowed my cereal slowly. I knew she'd notice sooner or later, but I wasn't sure how to explain it. I had decided the night Duffy went to the hospital that I would wear the

T-shirt for him to help him get well. He had told me to "use the enchantment," and I hadn't believed him. Well, maybe it was enchanted and maybe it wasn't, but I was going to give it a chance. I owed Duffy that much.

Finally I said, "It's kind of private, Mom. But I'm wearing it for Duffy, okay?"

Mom was silent for a moment, then she came over and roughed up my hair. "Of course it's okay. You know something, Heather? You're a very caring person, and I can't tell you how proud that makes me." I thought for a moment my mom was going to cry, and that scared me a little. Then she said, "Just do me a favor, okay? Wash it now and then?" and we both laughed and I knew it was all right.

Before she left for work, she said, "You know what I just thought of, Heather? It might be nice to send Mr. Duffy some flowers, since he doesn't have any family."

"Oh, Mom, could we?"

"Sure. Call up the flower shop in town. They'll deliver them. I've gotta go now." And she kissed me quickly on the forehead and left.

But a second later, she poked her head in the door again. "I take back what I said."

I looked at her blankly. "About what?"

"Your red hair. It's *not* the only thing you got from your dad. You also got his green thumb. I've been meaning to tell you, the backyard looks glorious!" And she was gone again.

I sat there for a while, beaming at what Mom had said, and thinking about ordering the flowers. But there was something that was keeping me from doing it. I didn't know what it was at first, and then I had it. Duffy would much rather have flowers from his own garden ... some of his "friends." Maybe some people would think it wasn't right to pick flowers out of his own garden, but I knew better. And I could bring them myself. It would be a long walk, but I knew where the hospital was. The flowers would help the enchantment, too.

I decided to call Lisa and ask her to come with me. I hadn't talked to her since that night, and I knew I had been kind of rude. Besides, it was well over a mile to the hospital and I didn't want to go by myself.

The phone only gave half a ring before it was picked up. There are so many Pringles around, somebody is always near the telephone.

"Hello?"

I could tell by the scratchy little voice that it was Harry.

"Could I speak to Lisa, please?"

"Who's this?"

"This is Heather."

"Oh. Hi, Heather."

"Hi, Harry."

There was silence for a moment.

"Harry, are you still there?"

"Yeah, I'm here."

"Harry, put Lisa on, okay?"

"Okay."

I heard the clunk of the receiver being dropped and then, off in the distance, "Li-sa!"

Finally, she picked up the phone. "Hello?"

"Lisa?"

"Oh, hi."

"Lisa," I began, "remember I told you that Duffy's in the hospital . . . ?"

"Who?"

Oh Lisa, I thought, don't start. Don't tell me you don't even know who Duffy is. . . . "Mr. Duffy," I said slowly. "Remember, I told you how I found him?"

"Oh, *him*," she said. "Yeah, how is he?"

"Well, that's why I'm calling you. It was a stroke. That's what he had, but he's going to be all right. And I'm going to pick some flowers out of his garden and bring them to him in the hospital. Will you come with me?"

"How are you going to get to the hospital?"

"I'm going to walk."

"All the way to the hospital?"

"Lisa, it's only a little over a mile. Come on."

"Let me see if my mother can drive us."

Before I could protest, she had put down the phone and gone off to ask her mother. I waited impatiently.

"She can't. She's got to take Bitsy to the doctor, and then she's got some other stuff to do in North Redbrook."

"Lisa, we can walk."

"No, I don't think so, Heather. It's too hot. And besides, I was over at Cathy Mercer's pool yesterday and I have a sunburn."

I had a queasy feeling in my stomach, but all I said was, "Okay, Lisa, good-bye."

"Bye," she said, and I let her hang up first.

I shouldn't have been surprised, but I was. Lisa never does anything she doesn't want to. So why should today be an exception?

I thought of asking Marshall if he wanted to come with me. He'd checked in with me every day to find out about Duffy. But I knew he was helping his stepfather paint an old sailboat they had bought. Marshall said when they had it fixed up they were going to take it out on Lake Cardigan, and he said I could go, too. I was glad it was working out between Mr. Teitelbaum and Marshall.

It was funny. At the beginning of the summer, I thought things had changed forever between Marsh and me. But I guess when you have a bond with someone, it never really changes. The thought slipped into my mind quietly: What had changed forever, maybe, was Lisa and me.

The phone rang and I was standing so close to it, with my mind so far away, that I jumped.

"Hello, Heather?"

"Mary?"

"Yeah! How are you? You haven't called, so I thought maybe you were away or something."

"Oh no, I've been right here." I told her about Duffy.

"Oh gee, that's awful. You must feel terrible." She sounded as if she really meant it.

"I did," I said simply. "But he's going to be all right."

"Oh, I'm so glad. Are you going to go and see him?"

"Well, I was going to. . . ." I told her about my plans to take the flowers from the garden. Then I said, "Too bad you don't live near me, maybe you could walk me."

There was a brief pause. "Gee, I'd love to. Wait a minute." She was back almost immediately. "Why don't we ride our bikes? I could meet you at the post office, and we could ride over to the hospital together."

"Hey, that's a great idea! I don't know why I didn't think of riding my bike." But of course I knew. Lisa never rode a bike; her mother said it was too dangerous. So I had gotten out of the habit.

"What time should we meet?"

I looked at the clock on the kitchen wall. "How about ten thirty. I gotta get up there and pick the flowers."

"Okay, see you at ten thirty at the post office."

When I hung up, I felt terrific. I grabbed my garden clippers and beat it up the hill to Duffy's place. It had rained yesterday, so I didn't have to worry about watering the garden. I had been coming up each day to feed Jezebel. She meowed like crazy each time I came in, and I know she wanted to go out, but I didn't think it would be safe. This way I would report to Duffy that she was safe and well-fed.

The garden looked beautiful as always. It was a breezy day, and the wild flowers in the meadow were bending this way and that like ladies in an exercise class. I remembered how still the meadow had looked the first time I saw it. Like a painting. . . . Fighting the urge to sit by the pond and just enjoy the sunshine, I picked hollyhocks, zinnias, lobelias, and a few daisies. Next time I could bring some from *my* garden. There weren't as many flowers, of course, so it would be a smaller bouquet, but that wouldn't matter to Duffy. When I got back to the house, I wrapped the bouquet in wet paper towels and then tightly in aluminum foil. Then I put the flowers in the basket of my bike, and I was on my way.

I got to the post office before Mary and stood straddling my bike, trying to catch my breath. It was all uphill from my house, and I was out of practice. A little boy with a Popsicle came out of the post office with his mother, and just as he got alongside me, half his Popsicle slid off the stick and fell to the ground with a *plop*. He stared at it for a moment, his lower lip quivering. But before he could decide to make a terrible scene, his mother had him by the hand and was hustling him off to their car.

I stood looking at the orange ice melt into the vanilla ice cream. I realized how dry my mouth was. I glanced around but I couldn't see anyplace where there'd be a water fountain or a soda machine.

"Hi!"

I turned to see Mary panting as I had been a moment ago.

"Hi!" I said.

She reached into her basket and took out a thermos. "Want some lemonade?"

"Do I! You must be a mind reader. I was just thinking how I'd die for a drink of something."

"My mom thought of this. I always get thirsty bike riding in this weather."

The lemonade tasted delicious, and as I handed her back the cup I said, "I really appreciate your doing this."

"Doing what?" she asked.

"You know, coming with me to the hospital."

"Don't be silly. What are friends for? I know I wouldn't want to go by myself. Hospitals give me the creeps."

We started down Longbranch Road, riding single file. It didn't take us long to get to the hospital, and we chained our bicycles up at the bike rack. I took the flowers out of the basket, and we started toward the front entrance. As we went up the steps, I smoothed down my Flower Power T-shirt and noticed I had dribbled some lemonade on it. I'd have to wash it out tonight.

The lady behind the desk was on the telephone when we went in, so we waited. My mouth felt dry, and I had butter-flies in my stomach. The only other time I had been in a hos-pital was when I sprained my ankle playing softball two years ago. I had come in through the emergency entrance and had it x-rayed.

"May I help you?"

The lady had hung up the telephone and was looking at Mary and me.

I leaned on the counter, keeping the flowers up in front of me so they wouldn't mess up her papers. "We're here to see Thomas Duffy. He's a patient here."

"How old are you?"

I stiffened. I had never thought about them not letting kids in. Before I could answer, Mary said, "Fourteen. We're both fourteen."

I started to glance at Mary, and then turned my attention back to Miss McCormack, as her badge identified her.

She pursed her lips and let out a sigh. "Are you sure you're fourteen?" she said, looking straight at me.

I stood as tall as I could and nodded my head. I didn't trust myself to speak. I had never been any good at lying.

"Just a moment, please," she said, and went over to con-sult a large file in the corner.

Mary nudged me. "I remembered when my grandmother

was in here two years ago. No one under fourteen is let in," she whispered.

Miss McCormack came back and looked at us disapprovingly.

"Mr. Duffy is in the intensive care unit. Only immediate family is allowed in."

"I'm his granddaughter," I blurted. I tightened my grip on the flowers and hoped she didn't notice my hand shaking.

Her face softened. "Well, I suppose it would be all right, just for a moment. And just you. Your friend will have to wait down here."

She filled out a slip of paper and gave it to me. "Take this elevator to the third floor, and give this to the nurse at the desk there."

I nodded, took the slip, and said "Thank you." Mary squeezed my arm and motioned to some orange chairs lined up against the wall.

"I'll wait right here," she said.

I went up in the elevator, getting more nervous by the minute. What if Duffy was connected to a lot of tubes and machines and looked just awful? What if he wasn't glad to see me? After all, I had deserted him. . . .

I gave the admissions slip to the nurse, and she silently led me down the hall and opened a door on my right. I was almost afraid to go in. When I did, what I saw immediately reassured me.

Duffy was lying in bed looking out at the trees. He had a tube in his arm, but otherwise he looked, well, he looked like Duffy. When he heard the door open, he turned and he broke into a big smile when he saw me.

"Hello, there," he said, and only his voice, a bit tired and shaky, reminded me that he was ill.

I went over and awkwardly held up the flowers. Miraculously, they hadn't wilted. "I brought these from your garden." His face lit up just as I knew it would when he saw his flowers. "My mother was going to send you some flowers from the store, but I knew you'd rather see your friends." The nurse was standing in the doorway, ready to put the flowers in water I suppose, and I wondered what she thought of our conversation.

"Miss Turner, this is Heather Mallory. Isn't she wonderful to bring me these?"

"I guess she thinks you're pretty wonderful, otherwise she wouldn't be here, right? You've a dear grandfather, Heather."

"Oh, Heather isn't . . ." but I seized his hand and squeezed it. He seemed to understand.

When Miss Turner left with the flowers, I said, "I had to tell them I was your granddaughter. I hope you don't mind. Otherwise they wouldn't have let me come up."

"Mind? Do you think I mind? I've never been so flattered." He was quiet for a moment. "I see you're wearing the T-shirt. Have you had any luck with it?"

"I think so. I've worn it since you got sick, and see how great you look! I think it *is* enchanted, Duffy. I think it really is." I wanted to tell him how things had changed for me. About Marsh, and Lisa, and Mary. But I knew I didn't have time now. Maybe later.

"I understand I owe you my life, Heather," he said, suddenly serious.

"Oh no, you don't."

"Yes I do. If you hadn't been my friend, and you hadn't come up to see me that day, I wouldn't be here now. And you know something, Heather? I'm very glad to be here. I didn't think it would matter. I thought I was ready to go. But I'm a selfish old man. I want every bit of life they can squeeze out of this old carcass!"

I smiled. "I'm glad. You look just swell. Oh, and I've been taking good care of Jezebel. But she misses you."

"Ah . . . Jezebel. She'd be a problem."

"What do you mean?" I asked.

"I have to decide, Heather, what I'm going to do. I have to make some changes in my life. We can't have a repeat performance, can we? What if you're not there next time?"

Miss Turner came in then. "I'm afraid time's up." She placed the flowers on a stand near the bed. "Can't tire Grandpa."

"You won't go away anywhere, will you?" I whispered, feeling afraid.

Duffy smiled and squeezed my hand. "Not if I can help it, Heather."

Before I left, I reached over and shyly gave him a kiss on his cheek. His skin felt very dry, and he still smelled of soap.

Mary and I bicycled back to the post office slowly.

"Let's get together tomorrow," she said. "My mom can pick you up, and you can have lunch at my house."

"I'd like that," I said. "And thanks again, Mary. I know it wasn't the most fun way to spend an afternoon."

Mary smiled. "Maybe you can come with me someday. I haven't seen my grandmother in ages."

I nodded, and we went in opposite directions. But I pedaled home feeling ridiculously happy. First, because it was all downhill, and second, because Mary understood about Duffy. I had a friend who felt like I did about things!

16

As Good as New

Duffy and I were standing under the weeping willow tree. The paper sparrow had long ago flown away, swept up by the same winds that had whipped the golden leaves from the trees and left Duffy's garden just a memory.

I looked up at his face as he drank in the familiar trees and shrubs and thought how right my mother was: Duffy seemed to have become younger since his illness. His face was thinner, but there was more color in it, and his eyes were even brighter than before.

Mom had taken a real interest in Duffy. She went to visit him in the hospital because, she said, if I found him so appealing then she must get to know him, too. It would be good for our relationship. She's been talking that way a lot lately, and I kind of like it.

"It's amazing," Mom said one day. "I mean, I never really knew him, of course, but I had no idea his mind was so alert. You should hear him carry on about the garbage fill they're planning for Robin's Cove! I'm going to drive him to the village hearing on that next month. He's really very well-informed, you know. He knows a lot more about ecology and the environment than I do."

"Duffy knows about a lot of things," I said proudly.

Dr. Barker had explained to Mom that sometimes senility is caused by the hardening of certain arteries, and there's not much they can do about it. I think that's what happened to Mary's grandmother. But lots of times what we think of as senility is caused by old people just withdrawing from the world. There's nothing of interest in it to them anymore, so they create their own world. I decided maybe that's why Duffy said his house was on the tour. I think he always wanted it to be, and he was only making believe. I *know* he never meant to lie to me, so I will never ask him about it. It just doesn't matter.

"I'm so glad you're back," I said to him now. "You are going to stay here, aren't you?"

He tightened his arm around my shoulder. "I hope so, Heather, I hope so. If I can get used to Sally, it should work out pretty good. Better than I expected a couple of months ago!"

As we spoke, I could feel Sally's presence in the background. She was a large woman with a pleasant, rosy face and blonde hair that she wore in two fat, waxlike pigtails. Sally was going to look after Duffy now. She would take care of the house, see that he took his medicine, and go with him for walks so that he got fresh air and exercise. Right now she was folding some lawn chairs and storing them in the cellar.

"I tried to tell Dr. Barker that if I *had* to have a companion, I'd like one of those young ladies I saw in the Miss America contest. But I suppose none of them were available. . . ."

I giggled. I wasn't just glad Duffy was home; I was relieved. For a while it looked like Duffy would have to go into Cedar Crest, the nursing home where Mary's grandmother is. I've been there twice now with Mary, and it's not a bad place at all. It's clean and new, and they have *lovely* gardens. Still, it wouldn't be the same. I wanted Duffy to be *here*.

I think Duffy knew how I felt, because one day when I was visiting him in the hospital he said, "You know, Heather, it wouldn't be so terrible if I went into Cedar Crest." I swallowed hard and tried not to show how upsetting I found the whole idea. "It's an excellent nursing home, and nursing homes are like hospitals, Heather: They're wonderful places to be when you need them. The thing that would be terrible would be if you were there only because nobody cared about you. *That* would be unbearable."

I felt a little better about it after that, and if Duffy ends up having to go there someday, I'll visit him the way Mary visits her grandmother. I think Mary feels better now. She goes and talks to her grandmother, and even if her grandmother doesn't answer, Mary says that half a conversation is better than none at all. Mary's not mad at her anymore. "You don't stop loving someone just because they're not perfect anymore," she said to me one day. I know what she means.

When Duffy went in for his nap, I helped Sally stack the cushions in the basement. We came back up the cement steps and stood for a moment enjoying the view. It was a cold, brisk day, and the sun was shining brightly.

"Pretty soon all the leaves will be gone," she said. "I always think this is the saddest time of year."

"I used to," I said, "with school starting and everything. But this year's been different."

"You like Mr. Duffy, don't you," she said, smiling at me. "He sure is a nice old gentleman. The nicest one I've ever worked for."

"He's almost like my grandfather," I said. "He really is in good shape for his age, don't you think, Sally?" I wanted her to tell me that it was a cold, undisputed medical fact: Duffy was as good as new. I wanted so much for that to be true. I think I was secretly afraid that Duffy had recovered only in my imagination.

"Heather, Mr. Duffy is in better shape than some men half his age," she said brusquely, wiping her hands on her apron as she started up the steps to the house. "Because up *here*"—and she pointed to her head—"and in *here*"—and she pointed to her heart—"he *is* as good as new." And she winked at me and went inside.

I decided I liked Sally. I wondered when Duffy would get around to telling her about her enchanted pigtails. He would. I just knew he would. And she would laugh and shake her head and not believe him.

But she'd learn, I thought happily, as I started home. Sally would learn.

 # About the Author

A native of New York City, *Sheila Hayes* counts gardening as one of the delights of her present home in Briarcliff Manor, New York. This enthusiasm spills over into *Speaking of Snapdragons*, her third children's novel. The author admits that she sometimes feels her garden, like the one in this story, is enchanted—but she concedes that her neighbors would probably use other adjectives to describe her efforts.

Mrs. Hayes is the author of *The Carousel Horse* and *Me and My Mona Lisa Smile.* She and her attorney husband have three daughters, all of whom have helped their mother to keep her sense of humor, if not her sanity, intact.